JUL 3 0 2003
P9-CKB-467

THE TIGER'S APPRENTICE

BOOK 1

ALSO BY LAURENCE YEP

GOLDEN MOUNTAIN CHRONICLES

The extraordinary intergenerational story of the Young family from Three Willows Village, Kwangtung province, China, and their lives in the Land of the Golden Mountain—America.

The Serpent's Children (1849)

Mountain Light (1855)

Dragon's Gate (1867)
A Newbery Honor Book

The Traitor (1885)

Dragonwings (1903)
A Newbery Honor Book

The Red Warrior (1939)
Coming Soon

Child of the Owl (1965)

Sea Glass (1970)

Thief of Hearts (1995)

DRAGON OF THE LOST SEA FANTASIES

Dragon of the Lost Sea

Dragon Steel

Dragon Cauldron

Dragon War

Sweetwater

When the Circus Came to Town

The Dragon Prince

Dream Soul

The Imp That Ate My Homework

The Magic Paintbrush

The Rainbow People

The Star Fisher

CHINATOWN MYSTERIES

The Case of the Goblin Pearls

The Case of the Lion Dance

The Case of the Firecrackers

EDITED BY LAURENCE YEP

American Dragons

Twenty-Five Asian American Voices

LAURENCE YEP

THE TIGER'S APPRENTICE

BOOK 1

HARPERCOLLINS*PUBLISHERS*

The Tiger's Apprentice

 Printed in the United States of America. For information address HarperCollins Children's Books, a division of HarperCollins Publishers, 1350 Avenue of the Americas, New York, NY 10019.
www.harperchildrens.com

Library of Congress Cataloging-in-Publication Data
Yep, Laurence.
The tiger's apprentice / by Laurence Yep. — 1st ed.
p. cm. — (The tiger's apprentice ; bk. 1)
Summary: A tiger, a monkey, a dragon, and a twelve-year-old Chinese American boy fight to keep a magic talisman out of the hands of an enemy who would use its power to destroy the world.
ISBN 0-06-001013-4 — ISBN 0-06-001014-2 (lib. bdg.)
[1. Magic—Fiction. 2. Chinese Americans—Fiction. 3. Orphans—Fiction. 4. San Francisco (Calif.)—Fiction.] I. Title. II. Series: Yep, Laurence. Tiger's apprentice ; bk. 1
PZ7.Y44Ti 2003 2002014413
[Fic]—dc21 CIP
AC

Typography by Andrea Vandergrift
1 2 3 4 5 6 7 8 9 10

First Edition

To Jesse, a wizard with a soccer ball

CHAPTER ONE

It isn't every day you meet a tiger. And certainly not a tiger in a suit and tie. And definitely not one who knows your first name.

The tiger was the last thing Tom Lee expected as he stumbled up the steps to his grandmother's home.

It was a grand old house in the Inner Richmond of San Francisco. Gingerbread shingles covered its sides like scales, and pigeons cooed under its ornate window eaves. It seemed to have cast some magical spell that protected it and its neighbors from being replaced by the cheap, ugly apartment houses that had swallowed up the rest of the city.

However, today, Tom didn't want to admire it. As he hurried up the steps, he just wanted to hide inside—away from all the people staring at the big bruise surrounding one eye and the torn sleeve of his blue shirt.

At the park Jack, an eighth-grader, had called Tom's

grandmother a weirdo—which everyone in the neighborhood did because of the way she decorated her house. It was full of magical charms—strange designs on paper, wood, and stone, and words written in a ghostly script. Hanging everywhere were mirrors with trigrams—sets of three lines, either solid or with a gap in the middle—from an ancient book called the Book of Changes. They made up patterns that could tell the future and had magical powers. And incense was always burning before bizarre statues.

When she walked down the street to do her shopping, their non-Chinese neighbors turned and whispered to one another. The Chinese in the area treated her as if she were invisible, and the Chinese shopkeepers were afraid to say a word to her and always waited on her first, as if they were in a hurry to get her out of their shops—not that she cared. She was proud of working magic and was even teaching Tom the rudiments of what she called the Lore.

Unfortunately for Tom, the neighborhood's attitude had filtered down to the children, who stuck Tom with the same label—weirdo. Bullies—Chinese or not—loved to pick on anyone different, and they had made Tom their favorite target.

He couldn't ignore an insult slung at his grandmother, who had taken care of him ever since he was a baby. His archaeologist parents had disappeared somewhere in Malaysia when he was only a year old. Everyone, including Tom and his grandmother, assumed they were dead.

Even though he was small for his age and his opponents were usually much larger, he defended his grandmother almost every day, and the frequent fights had earned him his own reputation as a troublemaker. His folder in the school counselor's office was stamped AT RISK.

So why should today be any different than any other day? Though Jack was an eighth-grader, Tom had demanded he take back his rude words. Of course, Jack wouldn't, and so there had been a fight. The real problem was that Jack had brought pals just as big as he was.

It would have been so much easier if Tom could have turned them into lizards, but his grandmother refused to teach him those spells until she was sure he would not misuse them. So Tom had had to use his fists. Against Jack alone, he might have stood a chance—which Jack knew and was why he had dared insult Tom's grandmother only when he had a gang around him.

"Turning them into lizards is too good for them. Fungus, maybe," Tom said to himself as the steps creaked under his feet. He couldn't wait to get inside the house. It was his fort, strange as it was. Within its walls, he felt safe from the rest of the world. And maybe he'd work on her again to teach him some spells he could use for defending himself.

At the door he fumbled for his key and found he had forgotten it. So he jabbed the doorbell hard. "Please, Grandmom. Hurry up," he muttered.

When the door opened, though, it was a stranger who

greeted him. "Good afternoon, Master Thomas. Your grandmother has been telling me wonderful things about you." The visitor took in the black eye and the torn sleeve and scratched his head. "But I see she might have been exaggerating a tad."

The stranger looked like an elderly man with a trim, gray mustache and goatee—except for his furry ears. The stranger brushed his goatee. "Do I have something on my face? Is that why you're staring?"

Tom's grandmother had taught him some basic spells, and one of them was for showing the true shape of things—which she said was essential for anyone working in magic. Curious about his grandmother's visitor, Tom chanted the words under his breath. He jumped when the next instant he saw a tiger standing there on his hind legs.

In the Chinese folktales his grandmother told him, animals could talk, but he had always thought those were just stories. He'd never expected to meet a talking animal.

"Is that you, Tom?" his grandmother called from the kitchen. "Where have you been?"

Suddenly Tom stood tongue-tied out of shame. He'd been so small when his parents had disappeared that he didn't remember them. Whenever Tom wanted a hug or a kind word, he could always count on his grandmother, but it was her voice he loved best. There was always a smile hidden behind her words. Her voice reminded Tom of a stream chuckling as it ran over rocks. He felt guilty for ducking out of his grandmother's lessons today, especially since he had run into Jack and his gang.

Impatiently the tiger slipped a watch from a pocket in his suit vest and consulted it. "I'd step inside unless you intend to eat on the porch. Mistress Lee, I think you'd better fetch Master Thomas if you don't want him turning into a porch fixture."

Tom's grandmother came out of the kitchen wearing an apron covered with stars. Her long white hair hung down her back in a heavy, braided rope. "Oh, my." His grandmother took Tom's arm and the tiger's paw. "You boys come inside this instant." Gently but firmly she pulled them into her house.

Once the door was shut, she rapped Tom on his forehead. "Why did you undo his disguise? What did I tell you about doing magic on impulse?"

Rubbing the sore spot, Tom began mechanically, "A moment's impulse leads—"

"—To a lifetime of regret," the tiger finished, and laughed, showing sharp fangs. "That was one of the first things your grandmother taught me as well, Master Thomas."

Standing on tiptoe, Mrs. Lee rapped the tiger on his forehead in turn. "I just wish you'd paid as much attention to your lessons on maintaining a spell. Look at you. It's a disgrace to let a beginner undo your transformation."

The tiger murmured a few words, and the next moment fur and fangs had disappeared and he was human again, including, this time, two very pink, embarrassed ears. "Am I more presentable now, Mistress Lee?"

"Tom, I'd like you to meet Mr. Hu, a former student of mine," she said, and smiled affectionately when she saw the tiger adjusting his orange-and-black-striped tie before the hallway mirror. "He's still quite the dandy."

Mr. Hu lowered his hands sheepishly. "You were the one who taught me to be careful of my appearance. Before you, I didn't care how tangled my fur was."

"And I never saw anyone take so to his lessons." Tom's grandmother laughed. "Some people might even think you were vain."

"Pleased to meet you," Tom said to the tiger politely.

His grandmother fingered Tom's torn sleeve and then noticed the yellow-and-blue circle around his eye. "Oh, dear, did you get into another fight?"

"They started it," Tom protested.

"Did you finish it?" Mr. Hu asked.

"No," Tom admitted.

Mr. Hu looked disappointed, but before he could make a comment, Mrs. Lee frowned disapprovingly at her visitor. "Hu!" And then she turned back to her grandson. "Tom, what have I always told you?"

"Violence—" Tom began.

"—Doesn't solve anything," Mr. Hu finished for the boy again. It was apparently another lesson that had been driven into his memory. "But I would be more concerned with the 'they.' You ought to show more sense about fighting battles when the odds are against you. That's simple mathematics."

Tom glanced at his grandmother accusingly. "It wouldn't matter if Grandmom would teach me some magic to defend myself."

"The Lore isn't for hurting people—no matter what the provocation." His grandmother frowned. "You have to learn the philosophy first."

"It's boring," Tom admitted.

"And so you got into trouble instead," his grandmother scolded him gently. "You shouldn't have snuck away from our lessons."

"I hated the theory too," Mr. Hu sympathized.

"Don't encourage him in his delinquency." Mrs. Lee wagged a finger at the tiger and then, unfortunately, turned her attention back to her grandson. "What was the fight about?"

"Nothing," Tom mumbled.

"You don't get a black eye over 'nothing.'" His grandmother stared at him hard until Tom began to squirm. It seemed to him sometimes that his grandmother threw some silent magic into those stares, but he could never be sure.

Tom looked down at his feet. "They said you were weird," he muttered.

His grandmother sucked in her breath slowly, as if the air hurt her lungs. "That's what children call anyone who's different," she said.

Mr. Hu eyed Tom critically and then grunted, "Don't worry, Master Thomas. These bullies are nothing compared to you. Forget them. You have a gift that the whole world will soon need."

"I do?" Tom asked, puzzled.

"Yes, and one that your grandmother will teach you to open," Mr. Hu said.

Tom's grandmother brushed Tom's hair out of his eyes with a hand that smelled very faintly of flour. "I just hope you pay more attention to your lessons than Mr. Hu did." She straightened the tiger's collar, then she began to straighten her grandson's clothes.

"Master Thomas is not a little doll," Mr. Hu said with a cough.

Mrs. Lee glanced sideways at the tiger. "Do I amuse you?"

Mr. Hu bowed quickly. "I mean no disrespect. I've just . . . never seen this side of you before."

Tom's grandmother made one last adjustment to Tom's clothing and then stepped back. "I was always so busy when my son was Tom's age; but by the time I realized that, Paul had already grown up. I'm not going to make the same mistakes now."

His grandmother looked so sad that Tom asked, "What mistakes, Grandmom?"

"Too many to mention," she said, tugging him down the worn boards of the hallway into the living room. The room had a high ceiling and elaborate molding that framed the doorways and windows and bookcases. But it was hard to see because of his grandmother's strange collections, including several odd swords hanging on the wall. The swords were made by stringing red cord through the center of old circular Chinese coins called cash. On one shelf was the prize of all her possessions—a coral rose that seemed identical to many sold in Chinatown souvenir stores; but his grandmother acted as if it were her most important thing in the world.

She gave Tom a gentle push toward the sofa. "Now you two boys get acquainted while I finish getting the tea ready."

Mr. Hu occupied the most comfortable chair, while Tom sat on the sofa as far away from him as he could get.

The tiger lifted a derby hat from the chair's seat and set it on a table. "I understand you're in the seventh grade, Master Thomas."

"Yes, sir," Tom said politely, even though what he really wanted to ask was what the tiger was doing here.

"Are you enjoying the summer?" Mr. Hu asked as he sat down. Tom's grandmother had only been making a suggestion that they become "acquainted," but the tiger seemed to take it as a command.

"Not exactly," Tom said, motioning to his eye.

"Ah, yes." Mr. Hu coughed. "I was always getting into fights when I was a cub too." Turning, the stranger studied his reflection in one of the many mirrors, brushing his goatee—which looked fine to Tom but was not perfect enough for the elegant Mr. Hu. "Fortunately I won more than I lost." He sounded a bit smug.

Tom eyed the tiger. "So you snuck out of Grandmom's lessons too?"

His sharp-eared grandmother must have overheard him because the clinks in the kitchen stopped abruptly. "Hu!" Tom's grandmother's warning floated along the hallway. "Be careful what you say."

Mr. Hu glanced nervously in her direction before saying, "Well, you'll find the theory is essential once you get into Elementary Sympathetic Magic."

Tom slumped on the sofa, suspecting how much more boring material he had to learn. "I wish I knew more than a few basics."

"Ah, but when the ground is prepared, you'll be ready for many exciting lessons." Mr. Hu chuckled as he reminisced. "Once, in Advanced Thaumochemistry, one of my potions went wrong, and I turned my fur and your grandmother's hair a brilliant purple."

Tom sat up eagerly. "What was the formula?"

"Hu!" Tom's grandmother scolded again from the kitchen.

The tiger threw up his paws apologetically. "At any rate, take my word for it: You'll find all this tedium worthwhile."

Tom hoped so. Right now, there were thousands of years of the Lore to be learned, and it seemed that every new fact drove an old one from his memory.

As Mr. Hu tried to find something safe to discuss with him, Tom had a chance to study the visitor. He looked normal enough now—except for something that flickered in his eyes like a flame in dry grass that could erupt into a wildfire at any time.

Soon Mrs. Lee appeared with a heavy tray floating behind her through the air. On it were meat and shrimp pastries that she made herself. They gave off the most mouth-watering scents.

"And for tea"—she triumphantly held up a small pot with a dragon on the lid—"Dragon Well."

Mr. Hu smacked his lips with pleasure. "You remembered my favorite."

"I've thought of you far more than you've probably thought of me," Tom's grandmother said. When she lifted her hand, the teapot rose as if on invisible strings and started to pour the liquid into the cups.

"There wasn't a day when I didn't think of my time with you." Mr. Hu leaned forward with his chopsticks to pick up one of the little meat pastries and set it on a small plate. "You were so kind and patient."

"You had great promise as my successor," Mrs. Lee said. Hurt was in her voice. "And yet you left."

The tiger threw back his head proudly. "I wrestled with the choice for days, but in the end I could not abandon my clan."

"A Guardian has no clan." She raised a finger, and the newly filled cup rose into the air and then let itself be guided over to the tiger. "You misused my lessons for your feud, didn't you?"

"Guilty." Mr. Hu raised his cup in one hand and the pastry with his chopsticks in the other. "They say a leopard cannot change his spots."

"Or a tiger his stripes." The disapproval was plain in her voice. "Well, are you finished?"

"The Jackals are a stubborn lot, but we finally got them to sue for peace. They won't trouble my clan for a long time." The tiger took a bite of his pastry and then a sip of his tea. "Ah, this is sheer heaven."

Tom heard an odd sound, like a truck motor idling. It took him a moment to realize that the visitor was purring.

"You were in a war?" Tom asked.

"Of a sort." Mr. Hu nibbled at the pastry happily. "My clan has been feuding with the Jackals for centuries, and there's many a Jackal who's sorry for that."

"The fight's been going on that long?" Tom asked in surprise.

"And why shouldn't it?" Mr. Hu asked, amused, as if war were as natural as a sunrise.

Tom wondered if Mr. Hu meant "jackals" figuratively or literally; he was going to ask, but his grandmother cleared her throat. "Force brings no true peace. Only a change of heart can."

"Which was the hardest lesson for me to learn—far harder than the calculus of chants. Fighting is in my blood," Mr. Hu said.

"Some of the greatest Guardians have been tigers," Mrs. Lee said as she sent a cup of tea through the air to Tom. "They managed to tame the fire in their blood and turn it to nobler purposes."

Mr. Hu smiled and shrugged. "I do not have their strength."

"And so you're going to sell antiques," she said, picking up a cup of her own.

Mr. Hu chuckled from deep within his throat. "I find it as humorous as you do, but my uncle left the store to me. And with the peace now, I have to make my living somehow. I expect I'll be bankrupt in six months."

Tom's grandmother arched an eyebrow and a shrimp pastry floated into her hand. "And so perhaps you'll be able to resume pursuing the Lore. Guardians have been known to train several apprentices at the same time."

Mr. Hu expertly balanced the tea on his free knee. "I am too old for lessons. Look at my fur. It's all grizzled with gray. Master Thomas will make a far better successor than I ever could."

"Tom's still young," his grandmother said, gazing at the tiger. "Why don't you just speak the truth? You no longer want to be the Guardian."

"You always understood my mind before I did." Mr. Hu

studied the ceiling thoughtfully, and when he lowered his head, he smiled. "But yes, I suppose I would like to end my days in peace. My fighting days are over."

Tom glanced at the coral rose, which his grandmother kept in a place of pride. He didn't see why anyone had to be the "Guardian" of something so ordinary.

"I just wish I knew why I was supposed to protect that," he wondered aloud.

The corners of Mr. Hu's mouth twitched up in a smile. "I can see you're as impatient as I was at your age."

Mrs. Lee laughed. "You two boys have more in common than a love of fighting."

"So when did you learn the secret?" Tom asked the tiger.

Mr. Hu turned respectfully to Tom's grandmother. "If Mistress Lee does not see fit to tell you, I don't see how I can."

"You'll learn all in good time," she promised.

But time had just run out.

CHAPTER TWO

There was a loud cracking noise from the hallway followed by a tinkling sound. Then another and another. Suddenly a magical mirror shattered near the doorway. Tom saw the shining shards fall to the floor.

The next instant a strip of yellow paper with red pictures burst into flame. Jumping to his feet, Tom tossed the tea from his cup onto it, but no sooner had he done that than a strip next to it caught fire. Grabbing a pillow from the sofa, Tom beat at it.

Mr. Hu had sprung to his feet but was crouching by the window, peering out. "Who could do this despite your defenses?"

"Something stronger than my wards, and that means it's very dangerous indeed." His grandmother rose and from a wall, lifted down a sword of coins threaded together. It collapsed for a moment in a copper tangle in her hand, but it took on its shape again when she held it pointed at the floor. Her other hand raised a wand of peachwood. "Take the rose and Tom. Leave by way of the roof. I'll make them think they've destroyed it."

"No! We can fight them off together," Mr. Hu insisted desperately.

Mrs. Lee's gentle voice suddenly became as sharp and hard as a dagger. It was as if the kindly grandmother he had always known had only been the sheath hiding the blade within. "This is my last command as the Guardian."

"But I am no longer your apprentice. I'm not listening to you!" Mr. Hu protested.

"You have the knowledge, and Tom is too young yet," Tom's grandmother said. "There is no one else to take my place right now."

Mr. Hu lowered his head as if it had suddenly grown heavy. "I'll avenge you."

"No, a Guardian cannot follow selfish desires like vengeance," Mrs. Lee said firmly. "You must protect the rose above all else." Her eyes softened for a moment when she glanced at Tom and she added, "And my grandson, who is just as precious to me."

Mr. Hu's voice choked. "I swear I will."

"Grandmom, what's happening?" Tom asked, bewildered. "Who's coming?"

"Go with Mr. Hu. Obey him as you would me. There isn't time for explanations." She wrapped an arm around him, and for a moment Tom could smell the warm kitchen scents that clung to her clothes. "But always remember: I love you, Tom."

His grandmother had been the one thing in his life he could be certain about—like the sun and the moon—with her treats and kind words. Tom clung to her tightly now. "But I don't want to go without you."

His grandmother shoved him away and used her stern voice again. "Don't argue."

Tom hardly recognized her. "What can you do alone? You should leave with us."

For a moment, his grandmother's voice grew softer. "These others will find more than they bargained for."

Her words didn't assure Tom, or Mr. Hu, who seemed almost at the point of tears. "Are you determined to stay?"

"Yes," Mrs. Lee said, and strode over to the shelves of curios. "I now pass this on to you."

With great solemnity she lifted the little coral rose from the shelf and held it out.

Clapping his derby on his head, the tiger took the rose reverently; when he spoke, his voice was husky with emotion. "I accept. But only temporarily until I can return it to you."

"Perhaps"—she smiled—"but if not, the burden will be yours."

The tiger shook his head sadly. "No, not this way . . ."

"You have your orders." She paced with great dignity to

the middle of the room, her braid swinging behind her back like a gray pendulum. "You'll find bags in the kitchen. Put the rose in one of those to hide it on the street." She had trouble trying to kneel because of her arthritis. "One last lesson to you: In the battles to come, trust your wits rather than your claws."

Tom tried to go to her, but Mr. Hu put a paw on his shoulder. "You mustn't distract the Guardian," he warned.

Bending, she began to trace patterns on the floor with her wand as she murmured strange words. Where the tip touched, the boards glowed with blue fire. In the intricate star pattern, strange curls and shapes began to appear and swirl about.

"Grandmom," Tom whispered, but she did not look at him, concentrating on the task at hand.

"Come," Mr. Hu said. As he pulled Tom out of the room, Tom glanced behind them.

His grandmother was now standing in the center of the fiery design, and as she raised the sword, it stood straight up, burning with a coppery flame.

"Hurry," Mr. Hu urged.

They stopped long enough to take a pink plastic bag from a neat pile in a corner of the kitchen. Reverently, Mr. Hu stowed the rose inside and then led them up the stairs. He seemed to know the house as well as Tom did, and he only slowed when they reached the last narrow staircase that led to the roof.

Glass crashed below them. Tom twisted on the step to go back, but Mr. Hu grabbed his arm. "You have your orders as well, Master Thomas," the tiger said.

"Let me go," Tom cried as he struggled to break free, but the tiger's grip was too strong. "I have to help Grandmom."

Mr. Hu bent over so Tom could look straight into his great amber eyes. "Listen to me, Master Thomas. This is not a playground fight against other boys. You can't help your grandmother against these kinds of enemies. You'll only be in her way if you go down there now."

Tom wanted to argue. But he didn't know much magic. He was willing to stand up to school bullies, but what could he do against whatever terrors were coming? Mr. Hu was right: Tom was useless.

The tiger drew the miserable boy up the remaining steps as thuds and thumps rose from underneath them.

Keeping hold of Tom with one paw, Mr. Hu unlocked the door and opened it a crack. He sniffed the air cautiously and his whiskers fanned out stiffly as he caught a scent. "Do exactly as I say, Master Thomas, or you'll die," he growled in a voice that was not to be disobeyed.

Tom kept glancing behind him back toward his grandmother. "Will she be okay?"

"Come," was all the tiger said, tucking the bag with the rose inside his vest. Then he opened the door a little wider, crouching as his eyes darted about.

Tom saw powerful muscles ripple beneath the tailored

cloth and daggerlike claws shoot out from the pads of the tiger's paws. When Mr. Hu dropped to all fours, the elegant dandy who had first greeted him had become the tiger he truly was—though still in his suit and hat.

Tom hesitated as the tiger slunk out onto the shingled roof. "Hurry, Master Thomas," Mr. Hu commanded in a low, powerful voice.

Telling himself that his grandmother trusted the tiger, Tom stepped out onto the shingles. Mr. Hu had no trouble slipping down the sharp slope, but Tom had to hold his arms out to balance himself. They had crossed halfway when Tom saw a thin black V appear on the shingles. It was the shadow of something—something that was coming fast as the V grew and grew.

"Don't look up. Keep going, Master Thomas," Mr. Hu whispered as his powerful shoulders tensed.

Tom forced his arms and legs to move, though they felt as stiff as a marionette's. Suddenly Mr. Hu snapped, "Duck."

As Mr. Hu dropped to his belly, Tom flung himself face-down. However, he couldn't resist turning his head to take a peek. What he saw made his mouth drop open.

A strange, twisted little man was plummeting down toward them. The man had an enormous bird's beak for a nose and cruel, beady black eyes. His huge feathery wings seemed to blot out the sun.

Tom had seen pictures like this in of one in his grand-mother's books and that had been scary enough, but nothing had prepared him for the real thing—the eyes burning with hate, the deadly talons and sharp beak.

As Mr. Hu's powerful legs sent him springing high into the air toward the monster, Tom saw a second shadowy V growing larger and larger. There were two of the creatures! And this one was diving from behind the unaware tiger.

Tom would have been willing to fight anything human; this was different. But Mr. Hu was his grandmother's friend. For her sake he had to do something.

Despite the fact he wanted to hide, the shamefaced boy forced himself to jump up, punching at the air. "Go away!" he shouted.

The second bird-man glared at him and from his mouth rose a bloodcurdling shriek. Tom flailed at the monster, but the great wings knocked him like a doll, first to the left and then to the right and then down the roof. He slid faster and faster until his feet struck the gutter. The trough broke from the fascia boards with a groan and a creak as the metal gutter bent, but it stopped his plummet.

At least, Tom thought, he had bought some time for the tiger. Mr. Hu slashed with his paw, and his claws sliced across the neck of the first creature. The tiger twisted his body in the air, letting the swing of his paw carry him in a half circle. As lithe as an Olympic gymnast, he struck the second creature in the throat. Tom cringed, expecting to be showered with blood, but where the creatures had been were now only fluttering pieces of paper. As a bit landed on a shingle, Tom saw that it was part of a cutout in the shape of the flying monster.

As he tried desperately to stop from sliding off the roof, Tom called over his shoulder, "Help me."

A growl answered him. Tom twisted his head and saw that Mr. Hu was still crouched on the roof, body tensed for another spring, fangs exposed, wild eyes searching for his next prey. All the gentlemanly manners had evaporated, leaving a wild beast in a costume that could barely contain his powerful body.

Astonished, Tom stared at Mr. Hu as, ears flattened against his skull, the tiger's eyes hunted the skies for enemies as deep, deadly growls rumbled from his belly. But then, as his gaze swept over the rooftop, he finally caught sight of the boy about to go over the edge. With a great effort, he relaxed his body and raised his head, his ears rising up again. "I'm . . . I'm—" the tiger seemed to struggle to remember how to speak "—I'm coming, Master Thomas."

He padded easily down the shingles and extended a paw; when Tom just stared at it with wide eyes, the tiger grew impatient. "Hurry up. What's the matter?" The tiger glanced down and then said sheepishly, "Oh." He retracted the claws into the pad.

With no other choice Tom reluctantly took the paw and let himself be pulled up beside the tiger.

"What were those things? Paper dolls?" Tom asked, bewildered.

"To be more exact, they were imitations of a monster, but just as deadly." With swift swipes of his claws, he shredded what was left of the paper. "Now hurry."

His grandmother had mentioned monsters and the darker magic, but she had never gone into detail, concentrating instead on the basics that Tom was to master. So until then magic had seemed more like a hobby.

Numbly, he stumbled after the tiger, who was crossing the roof to a fire escape. Glancing around, Mr. Hu began to descend the rungs. Tom felt dizzy as he looked down the three stories.

Mr. Hu glanced up anxiously. "We mustn't waste the time that your grandmother is purchasing for us."

Tom turned around so his face could be to the wall. Then he stuck out a foot and groped blindly for the first rung.

"For heaven's sake, don't take all day!" Mr. Hu growled. Tom almost screamed when he felt the tiger seize his foot in a paw, but Mr. Hu was only guiding it to the ladder.

As he climbed down, Tom tried to look straight ahead of him at the wall boards rather than below. Somehow he made it to the alley, which was so narrow that the tiger had to slide along sideways after he had disguised himself once again as a human gentleman.

"I'm getting too old for this," Mr. Hu groaned when they were on the street, and he swung one arm in a slow circle. "I'm going to be sore tomorrow. And I'm not as quick as I used to be. In my youth I would have been more watchful and not let another enemy sneak up on me when I was distracted by the first." When Tom started to head for the nearest house, the tiger grabbed his shoulder. "Not that way. We need to leave this spot."

Tom pulled away. Now that he had seen the powerful tiger in action, he wouldn't have stood near him any more than he would have gone into the tiger cage at the zoo. "I'll go and call the police."

Mr. Hu clutched the bag tightly in one hand. "Your grandmother doesn't want that any more than the thieves do. We have to put as much distance between ourselves and the house as possible. Besides, what do you think they could do against our enemies?"

Tom thought of the flying monsters. He wasn't sure. "So what do we do?"

"We get the rose to safety," the tiger said. "And then we plan our revenge."

There was something in the determined way that the tiger spoke that made the boy shiver. Mr. Hu seemed quite comfortable with feuds, and Tom had seen how easily the wild beast could appear.

Still, Mr. Hu seemed less dangerous than the monster on the roof, so Tom might as well take the tiger's advice for now. He forced his legs to move down the street, but he couldn't help looking back over his shoulder, wondering what was happening to his grandmother.

A thick column of smoke twisted into the sky like a giant gray snake; in the billows, Tom saw flashes of light and stripes of white smoke.

"Yes, Mistress Lee," Mr. Hu murmured with satisfaction, gazing back over his shoulder as well. "Make them sorry they came without an invitation. And then join us."

Suddenly a blinding bolt of light sliced through the column straight up to the sky.

Tom's eyes were dazzled by the bright light. He thought he saw a giant moth flapping pale gray wings with brown spots that looked like skulls. It circled several times over the spot where his grandmother's house had been and then soared upward into the sky.

Mr. Hu's voice thickened with shock and sorrow. "The Ghost Cart . . ."

"You mean the moth?" Tom asked.

"It comes for the souls of the brave and noble and good," Mr. Hu said, gazing at the sky and choking for a moment. "Like your grandmother."

The last few minutes had felt like some horrible nightmare from which Tom would wake up, but suddenly he realized he would never see his grandmother again.

"Grandmom . . ." There would be no more smiles, no more hugs, no more gentle words.

Tom was so full of grief, he forgot to be afraid of the tiger. Turning, he threw himself against Mr. Hu and began to cry.

The pungent smell of sandalwood filled his nose as he

pressed his face against the tiger's suit.

The tiger lifted a paw and patted the boy clumsily on the back. "Remember your grandmother's sacrifice, Master Thomas. This is what Guardians must do: protect that most precious object with their lives, even though few know of it. For thousands of years, we have kept it—and the world—safe."

His grandmother had thought the rose so important that she had given her life for it. "But who's the Guardian now?"

"I am," Mr. Hu said solemnly. "And since I now stand in your grandmother's stead, you are now my apprentice. Don't worry. It will be your turn someday."

CHAPTER THREE

The flying rat has the body of a hare but the head of a rat. It flies through the air by moving the hairs along its back.

—Shan Hai Ching

Even though he was stunned, Tom felt as if someone had just shoved an icicle against his back. He pushed away from the tiger. "I . . . I don't think I want to be a Guardian anymore," he said. "Grandmom told me about the monsters, but it's not the same as meeting them."

"No one could really prepare you," Mr. Hu admitted, "but fighting them is in your blood. As Mistress Lee's grandson, it is both your heritage and your duty. You are part of a long tradition that keeps the rose safe."

The mention of his grandmother made Tom hesitate for a guilty moment, but the terror was still too fresh in his mind. "No, you're the Guardian now. You choose your own apprentice." Besides, after seeing Mr. Hu's transformation into a wild beast, the tiger seemed almost as dangerous as the monsters. "You don't want me. You said it yourself back on the stairs: I'm useless against monsters. I don't have the magic or the claws."

The tiger gazed at the frightened boy almost as if he could see right through his skin to his insides. After a moment, the tiger nodded. "But you have the courage. It takes a brave heart to face creatures such as the ones on the roof without weapons."

"And get knocked over like a bowling pin." Tom winced. He was sure his arms and legs were bruised.

Mr. Hu clasped his hands behind his back. "I said you couldn't stand up to such invaders—yet; but with training you can. Your grandmother saw the worth in you. And she was among the wisest of creatures. I can do no less than follow her judgment."

"She was my grandmom. And I only went along with the lessons because she wanted me to." And now, the only one who loved him was gone. Tom felt like crying all over again. "Now that I know what I've gotten into, I don't want to anymore."

As he stared at the frightened, miserable boy, the tiger seemed lost for a moment—as if he didn't have the slightest notion of what to do with a human cub. "I'm afraid you have no more choice in being my apprentice than I have in being the Guardian. So come, Master Thomas. We must both obey your grandmother's last commands. But first let's clean that face."

Tom glanced at his reflection in a grocery store window and saw that when he had fallen on the rooftop, his face had gotten filthy. Pulling a red silk handkerchief from his coat breast pocket, Mr. Hu began to wipe the dirt away.

"Ow," Tom complained at the rough scrubbing.

"I'm sorry. I see that human cubs are less durable than tiger ones." Embarrassed, Mr. Hu handed the handkerchief to Tom.

"Do you have children?" Tom asked.

"No, between my studies and then the feud, I never had time to court anyone," Mr. Hu explained brusquely. "But when I was with my clan, there were always cubs underpaw."

Tom studied his face in the window as he began to wipe his cheeks. He had his father's eyes with the epicanthic fold but his Irish mother's pale skin and brown hair. His didn't look like the face of someone who could stand up to monsters.

When Tom tried to return the handkerchief to Mr. Hu, the tiger waved it away. "I don't want it back in that state. Put it in your own pocket, if you please. You can wash it out later."

Tom had expected Mr. Hu to work some magic to whisk them away, so he was surprised when they caught a bus that rolled past the stores and apartment houses lining Geary Boulevard.

"Shouldn't we get away as fast as we can? What if the monsters find us?" Tom whispered.

"They won't be looking for us," Mr. Hu said. "They'll think the rose was destroyed with your grandmother. But if by some chance they see us, they'll think we've just been shopping." He held up the pink bag with the rose.

On Market Street they got off among the tall department stores and office buildings. Tom felt as if he was in a deep stone canyon in which people in suits hurried back and forth in the twilit streets.

Lounging against the wall of a high-rise, bike messengers sat waiting for errands.

"You're back, partner," a high, nasal voice called.

At first Tom had missed the creature among the bigger humans until he padded toward them waving a paw. He was about two feet high, but his yellow fur was so bushy that it was hard to tell if he was fat or the hairs were long. On his head was a cap with furry flaps, and his feet were so large that they almost seemed like a rabbit's.

Mr. Hu's nose wrinkled as if he had just smelled something very unpleasant. "You're still alive."

"So are you." The rat grinned.

Mr. Hu glowered. "In the past I may have used your services, but only when I had no choice. That does not make us partners and never will."

The rat nudged Tom's leg. "He's a great kidder, is my Mr. H."

Mr. Hu bent over until his nose was almost touching the rat's snout. "Go away, Sidney, or I will be forced to bite you—even if I'll be rinsing with mouthwash for a month afterward."

Sidney took no notice of the angry tiger as he pulled a business card from out of his fur and handed it to Tom. "The name's Sidney Stillwater, and who might you be?" he asked, holding out his paw.

Tom stared down at the pink palm with its tiny, fingerlike claws until he realized the rat was expecting Tom's business card in return.

"Tom Lee," the boy said, and patted his pants pocket apologetically. "I'm afraid that I don't have any cards."

"No kidding," Sidney said. Snatching his card back from Tom's fingers, the rat pivoted back to Mr. Hu. "So what've you been up to lately, Mr. H?" He lowered his voice. "Something important, I bet. Come on. You can tell your old partner."

"We are not—and never have been—partners, and it is none of your business," Mr. Hu declared firmly. "Now, good day."

However, Sidney stayed with them as they walked along, wheedling, joking, and even begging on his knees once for information. He ignored all requests to leave them alone and apparently did not believe any of the tiger's threats, no matter how dire. He did not stop talking even as he nimbly dodged a blow by darting behind Tom's legs. The boy noticed that the tiger had only used the flat of his hand, so he had not meant the rat any great harm.

Finally an exasperated Mr. Hu gazed up at the sky. "Give me strength," he muttered.

"Anything for my partner." Sidney beamed, and from within his fur, he brought out a small blue bottle. "This strength tonic will pep up a skeleton, so it ought to work real good on a big strapping tiger like you. It's normally twenty bucks, but for you I'll make it five."

The tiger pounced on the rat, seizing him in his paws. "Sidney, I—"

At that moment they heard a chirping sound. "Hold that thought, Mr. H. I'm being paged." Wriggling out of Mr. Hu's grasp, Sidney reached into his fur and pulled out a cricket that was rubbing its legs together frantically. The rat studied the position of the cricket's antennae. "Oops. That must be the job I was expecting. Got to go pick up a package. Sorry, partner, we'll have to catch up later."

Tom was expecting the rat to head back for a tiny bike, but after stowing the tonic and cricket away, Sidney just stood there and squeezed his eyes shut. Suddenly he seemed to puff out like a furry balloon. At first Tom thought he had inflated himself, but then he realized it was just the rat's hair standing on end.

When only the tip of his snout and his pink paws showed, the rat's outline began to blur and Tom heard a soft, humming sound. Tom felt his own skin tingling; then, with a start, he saw the rat's hair was vibrating all along its back.

Slowly the shimmering rat rose straight up into the air like a helicopter. "Catch you later, Mr. Hu. Nice to meet you,

Tom." With a nod, he soared rapidly along the sidewalk, darting in and out through the crowd.

As Sidney soared out of sight, Mr. Hu warned his apprentice, "Never let that rat inside your home. He'll stay for weeks." He sounded as if he spoke from experience.

Tom glanced around at the jammed sidewalk. "But he's not in disguise."

Mr. Hu shrugged. "Sidney doesn't have that kind of magic."

Tom scratched his head. "But don't people see he's a talking, flying rat?"

"You'll find most people will see what they want to see. And what they see is a short little bike messenger in a fur coat and cap." Mr. Hu nodded to the other bike messengers, who were dressed more outrageously than the rat. "Bike messengers are invisible."

"But he flew," Tom pointed out.

"He's careful to stay at skateboard level," Mr. Hu said, "and people are so busy dodging Sidney, they don't look down to see if he really has a skateboard. Besides, he's gone before they can say anything."

"Are there many others like him?" Tom asked. "I mean, animals that talk?"

"Like me, you mean?" Mr. Hu arched an eyebrow. "Of course. The whole world loves to come to San Francisco to live. In a place with so many different types of people, who would notice a few who are a little more 'unique'? If humans like to live in San Francisco, why not magical creatures? You will find griffins from Wales, *garudas* from India, trickster mantises from Africa. They all come here because of the *ch'i*."

Tom remembered his studies. "That's like a kind of energy, isn't it?"

Mr. Hu shaped an invisible pipe with his fingers. "It flows through the world along channels just as blood flows through your body along arteries. There are some spots where there are many lines of it, and San Francisco is one. Anyone with magic would be drawn here."

Wondering what they were going to meet next, Tom followed the tiger as he turned up Grant Avenue. In the distance Tom glimpsed the tiled roofs of Chinatown and the bright neon signs with the Chinese characters.

"We're going to Chinatown?" Tom asked.

"Where else?" Mr. Hu asked, as if there were no other place in the world for a proper tiger.

The sidewalks were crowded with people, many of them tourists shivering in shorts and T-shirts because of the mistaken idea that San Francisco should be warm in the summer. No one took any more notice of the tiger here than they had on Clement Street. As Tom passed the fish swimming in tanks in a store window, the day felt even more like a dream.

In the window of one souvenir store, he saw coral roses to match his grandmom's. Some of them were attached to cheap bracelets. Others were meant to be worn as brooches.

They lay scattered among the souvenir ashtrays and model cable cars. There were also fake ivory objects made out of white plastic as well as some made of a transparent yellow material.

"Don't dawdle, Master Thomas," Mr. Hu said.

"I was just wondering what that stuff was," Tom said, pointing at some jewelry made from a translucent yellow stone.

Mr. Hu said with a frown, "It's amber."

"Did I say something wrong?" Tom asked.

Mr. Hu looked away quickly. "I see your grandmother never explained. There is amber that comes from the sap of ancient trees."

"Like in the dinosaur movie where they got the DNA for the dinosaurs," Tom said, remembering.

Mr. Hu did not look as if he had seen many movies. "And then there is the other kind of amber that is made from the souls of tigers. It's very powerful. I don't like to see that sold as if it were just a trinket."

Tom stared at the window, horrified. "Is any of that here?"

"No," Mr. Hu said, "it seems like the tree kind, or"—he peered closer—"imitations made from resin."

He seemed in a hurry to leave the store behind, though, and Tom followed him. Pungent smells came from a herbal shop, and Tom rubbed his nose. "That stinks."

They went by more souvenir stores selling roses almost identical to his grandmother's until the tiger finally ducked into a narrow alley where the buildings crowded forward as if trying to swallow up all the space. The sun could not reach here, so it seemed to be forever in twilight and shadow.

Tom wasn't expecting to halt, so he almost bumped into the tiger when he stopped by a dark brick building. On the street level was a store with a sign that said ART AND CURIOS.

Taking out an ornate iron key, Mr. Hu opened the door. Tom's nose wrinkled at the dusty smell. "When was the last time anyone cleaned in here?"

"Quite a while. My uncle was long dead before I got the news I had inherited it," Mr. Hu said.

Mr. Hu's store was just as odd as Tom's grandmother's house. On the walls were mirrors of all sizes with frames covered in Chinese words and different patterns of lines. Beside them dangled yellow scrolls with more Chinese words written in bright red. Some words Tom recognized, but some were little better than scrawls. Other scrolls had strange pictures and diagrams.

The floor was crammed with antiques of all kinds. Massive teak cabinets loomed over painted porcelain cylinders a yard high. "What are those?" Tom asked, tapping the ceramic top of one.

Mr. Hu brushed his hand away. "That drum stool is for sitting in the garden, not for playing. But don't dawdle, Master Tom. We have much to do."

Tom pivoted slowly. Red lacquer snuff bottles lay jumbled on one shelf next to ivory carvings. "It's like a museum in here."

"And you'll get to know every part of it when you dust it." The tiger hurried past the furniture and shelves to a door in the rear, and Tom followed him through it into a small apartment that seemed to double as a workroom. A table against the wall was covered with jars of glue, cans of varnish, and brushes with sticky bristles. Against another wall was a small vault.

"That looks like it belongs in a bank," Tom said.

"This store used to be a jeweler's," Mr. Hu explained. "And my uncle was never one to waste anything."

In the middle of the floor was a chair whose legs were tied with string and little vises. The tiger must have been repairing it for sale outside.

But everything here, too, had a layer of dust.

The tiger ignored the chaos as he reverently drew out the coral rose from the bag. "Behold your destiny, Master Thomas."

CHAPTER FOUR

Kung Kung is a snake with a human face and red hair.
—Shan Hai Ching
(Kung Kung is also referred to sometimes as the first rebel.)

As a child, Nü Kua spent most of her time cutting wood near her parents' home. When her brother became emperor, he summoned her; and when he died, she succeeded him. She had great power and wisdom and ruled the people well.
—Chinese tradition

Tom stared and stared, trying to see something special about the rose. "It's just another Chinatown souvenir. Why did Grandmom have to die for that?"

"Because it is something that must never fall into the wrong hands—or claws, as the case may be." Cradling the rose reverently in his paw, the tiger walked over to a table. Its legs were long and slender, and strange diagrams and symbols decorated their length and the top. Taking a domed glass case from the floor, he placed it gently over the rose.

"But what is it?" Tom demanded, still feeling the ache inside that his grandmother was dead. "I want to know what I'm supposed to fight for."

Mr. Hu polished the glass dome covering the rose while he thought for a time. Finally he straightened. "Yes, considering what's happened, I suppose I owe you that. What do you know of Chinese history?"

"Grandmom didn't get to that yet, but in school I read about an emperor who built the Great Wall," Tom said.

Mr. Hu's whiskers twitched in amusement. "That emperor was a youngster compared to the empress I'm talking about. Many millennia before him, Nü Kua ruled China." He spoke the name softly—as if afraid of being overheard.

"Who's Nü Kua?" Tom asked, feeling more ignorant than ever—and yet also feeling that what he didn't know might get him killed.

Raising a claw, Mr. Hu made a hushing sound. "A wise person speaks her name as little as possible, Master Thomas."

"Does she have spies around?" Tom asked.

"Even the Lore can't describe all of her powers. It may be she can overhear us." The tiger even glanced around cautiously before he resumed. "She was perhaps the greatest and wisest and most powerful of all the rulers of China. I can see we have a great deal to cover. Well, what do you know about the *Feng Huang*?" When Tom looked blank, the tiger explained, "Westerners would call it the phoenix."

"I've read all about them," Tom said, trying to impress Mr. Hu. "They're reborn in fire."

Mr. Hu chuckled. "I don't know where westerners come up with such preposterous things. There is no fire involved. The phoenix is far greater and more beautiful. He is one of the Four Supreme Creatures, and he is the king of all winged things and has the gift to transform evil hearts into good ones. Once long ago when the world was new, there was a Minister of Punishments known as Kung Kung."

"Who's Kung Kung?" Tom asked.

"A creature with terrible powers," the tiger explained, "but still not as great as the Empress's. Kung Kung was very strict about the laws, so strict that no one—dragon, spirit, or human—could live up to them; but he was harshest on humans. He objected to the way they multiplied and spread over the land. He wanted to limit them and for them to know their place. Finally he became so exasperated that he wanted to use the phoenix to force everyone to obey, but the Empress refused because she said what was happening was heaven's will. So he raised the banner of rebellion, and he was only stopped after much death and suffering and destruction."

"Why didn't the Empress use the phoenix to stop him?" Tom wondered.

Mr. Hu seemed shocked. "Magic that forces someone to change taints itself. It poisons the heart of the user. The Empress understood that, where Kung Kung did not. Once Kung Kung was defeated, the phoenix himself decided that this was not the proper age for him and returned to an egg, for he has that ability as well. And the Guardians were created to protect the phoenix in his slumbers. So that its powers cannot be misused, the phoenix must only wake in times of peace."

"When you don't really need it anyway." Tom stared at

the simple coral rose as the news sank in. If it really had that kind of power, he was beginning to understand why his grandmother would die defending it. "If this is really an egg, why does it look like a flower?"

"It's in disguise, just as I am," Mr. Hu said, placing a hand upon the dome. "Since the first Guardian hid it as a grain in a bushel of rice, it has been the right of his or her successors to choose the shape it will have."

For a moment the red petals seemed to become translucent as glass, and Tom thought he glimpsed something dark swimming inside. Quickly he muttered the spell he had used to see Mr. Hu's true shape, but this time the coral rose remained as it was.

Mr. Hu was amused. "You'll need more than that to break its disguise. Your grandmother protected it with the strongest, most complex spells."

"Well, how did the phoenix egg get here?"

Mr. Hu regarded the rose somberly. "Though Kung Kung was destroyed, some of his rebels, who call themselves the Clan of the Nine, survived; and they have been attempting to carry out their lord's original plan ever since. Throughout China's long history, they have pursued the phoenix, and for just as long a time we Guardians have kept it out of their paws; but a hundred and fifty years ago, China was wracked by war and rebellion. It was too dangerous for the egg to stay, and the Guardian at that time became so desperate that he brought it to America."

Tom wrapped his arms around himself. "Why here?"

"This country was safer at the time," Mr. Hu explained. "And the Guardian was able to hide himself among the many Chinese who emigrated to work here."

"And Kung Kung's rebels followed him too?" Tom asked.

"If human gangs could come from China, why not truly evil creatures as well?" Mr. Hu clasped his hands behind his back. "Do you think ordinary humans were the only ones who had reason to travel to America? For the last century and a half, Kung Kung's rebels and their descendants have been searching the four corners of the earth. The fact that they haven't found the egg until now speaks well of that immigrant Guardian's wisdom to leave China."

"How many more of them are there?" Tom asked with a gulp.

Mr. Hu scratched his throat. "I don't know their numbers, but they will be coming here from all over the whole world now that they have located it."

Tom was almost sorry he had found out what the rose was. Now that he knew what power it really had and what kinds of creatures were seeking it, he was even more scared. "I wish Grandmom had told me so I had a choice about being her apprentice. I'm the last one who could save the world."

"She was probably afraid of just this kind of response," Mr. Hu said, watching him. "I'm sure she was waiting until you were stronger and more confident in your magic so you would feel ready to take on this burden. There were other apprentices after me and before you; all of them failed for one reason or another. The secret is too great to entrust to just anyone."

"Then why did you tell me?" Tom asked.

"She kept you in ignorance because the times seemed quiet and safe. However, now that our enemies have found us, I can't expect you to follow this path blindly and on faith," Mr. Hu said. "Had Mistress Lee lived, I believe she would have revealed the truth as well."

The rose seemed so small that it was hard to believe it could change the world. The light shining on the petals' edges curved like ominous smiles. With a shiver, Tom wondered if he would be better off in a foster home. At least he'd be with his own kind rather than with a tiger.

When he turned around, he found Mr. Hu had begun to write out words and diagrams in red ink on long yellow strips of paper.

"Grandmom's charms didn't work," Tom pointed out. "Why should those?"

"Because she didn't have time to put up wards as strong as I will," Mr. Hu said. "And because she dwelt above only a single line of *ch'i*. But my store is where several such channels intersect. That makes this place far more powerful."

"Why didn't Grandmom move?" Tom wondered.

"For a long time things have been relatively peaceful," Mr. Hu said, fanning the paper to dry the ink faster, "so one line of *ch'i* probably seemed sufficient. And Mistress Lee loved that house."

"She used to talk to it as if it were a friend," Tom said.

"Perhaps it was, in a way." Mr. Hu shrugged.

"And the charms will tap into the *ch'i*?" Tom asked.

Mr. Hu held up the paper so Tom could see what he had done. "Yes. Think of it as my own security system. It will be even better than burglar alarms and vaults against the kind of thieves we now face."

The tiger half drew and half wrote more of the charms. Leaving the others to dry, he taped a couple of the still-wet ones on the wall. Tom's first job as an apprentice was to hold the tape.

When they had set them all up, Tom said, "That doesn't seem very hard."

Mr. Hu looked at him, annoyed. "The hardest part is yet to be done. To activate the charm takes a good deal of the soul."

Leaning forward toward a paper charm, he muttered a spell and breathed on it. Tom's eyes widened as the red letters glowed like fire. Mr. Hu's shoulders sagged as if he had just run a mile, and he grew more and more tired as he repeated the magic. By the time all the charms were glowing like small neon signs, he could barely stand.

Mr. Hu had moved so powerfully upon the roof that Tom had forgotten how elderly the tiger really was. Looking at the silver tips of the Guardian's hair, Tom felt sorry for him.

"You should sit down," he said, trying to take the tiger's elbow.

Mr. Hu shook him off. "I'll be fine in a moment."

But the aged tiger took his time shuffling into the rear apartment and didn't object when Tom held out a chair. "It does take a bit out of me," he confessed.

He had left one charm on the table, next to a pouch embroidered with a bird that had long, red, fiery tail feathers. "This is what the phoenix looks like," Mr. Hu explained, and tucked the last charm into the pouch. Then the tiger slipped the pouch's long string over Tom's head and lowered it so it dangled down Tom's chest. "There is power even in his symbol. It should help keep you safe from minor pests like the monsters on the roof."

When Tom tucked the charm inside his shirt, he felt a sudden warmth and a tingle, as if it was alive. Then, at Mr. Hu's direction, he got a bottle of black ink, a new brush, and a couple sheets of paper.

Tom watched curiously as Mr. Hu began to write words in the same strange script as before.

"More charms?" Tom asked.

"No, I'm writing two friends for help." Mr. Hu paused, nibbling at the end of the brush as he thought what to put down next.

"Do you need envelopes?" Tom asked, looking around the room.

"No, just matches." Mr. Hu chuckled. Writing rapidly,

he signed the first letter with a flourish and then waved a paw at a different table. "I think I left some there."

Tom fetched them for the tiger and waited for Mr. Hu to copy the letter again. Then, striking a match, the tiger held up one of the letters. Tom's puzzlement changed to surprise when Mr. Hu set fire to it. Flames shot up the paper. As the tiger released it, the letter disappeared in a puff of smoke.

"What are you doing?" Tom stepped back in alarm, thinking fire was especially dangerous with all the cans of paint and varnish in the room.

Mr. Hu set fire to the second. "You could say I am mailing them."

Tom couldn't imagine who or what could read a letter that way. "And your friends will come?"

Mr. Hu nodded toward the rose. "They'll come to protect that."

Tom circled the case. "Are you sure?"

"They know I would summon them only in dire need." Mr. Hu swept a few ashes into his paw.

Tom had no sooner put away the inks than smoke suddenly gathered before the tiger's nose, making him sneeze.

Quickly the smoke solidified into a long, narrow piece of paper. "Ah, a reply already." Mr. Hu snatched the letter from the air. He glanced at it and said with satisfaction, "She's nearby. How convenient. Fetch my hat, Tom. We're going for a stroll."

As Tom got the hat and handed it to the tiger, he jerked

his head at the rose. "What about that?"

"Our attackers are probably still waiting until the authorities leave your grandmother's house so they can sift through the ashes. And that will take a while. If we can get help, it's worth the risk." Mr. Hu crumpled the letter into a ball and it vanished back into smoke. "It wouldn't be a bad thing either to familiarize yourself with your new territory. And we can get you some clothes."

"Where are we going?" Tom asked, wondering what stores would be open this late.

The tiger set his hat on his head and studied its angle in a mirror. "To Goblin Square," he said, making a final adjustment. "Where else would you shop?"

CHAPTER FIVE

"I've never heard of Goblin Square," Tom said as they left the store.

"I'm surprised Mistress Lee never took you there," Mr. Hu said as he locked the front door. "There is a whole hidden city within San Francisco, but you must know the paths and doors that lead to its various parts."

Under the light of the streetlamps, people with large plastic bags of food were rushing home. Mr. Hu took Tom past ornate Chinese buildings and down narrow alleys. The air was filled with mouthwatering smells as people began to cook dinner, and Tom remembered that he'd had nothing since the tea.

As they walked through Chinatown, Mr. Hu began more of Tom's lessons. "Now listen to me and you will live. The first thing is to know the territory in which your battles will be fought." He told Tom about the streets and alleys as they passed through them. The tiger's pride in Chinatown was plain as he told Tom of the legends and local gossip.

"I thought you just came back to San Francisco?" Tom asked.

"But I lived here for many years before you were born," Mr. Hu explained.

"Did you know my father?" Tom asked.

"Yes, but he was still a small cub when I left," Mr. Hu said. "At the time I assumed he would become the next Guardian, so I thought it safe to answer my clan's summons."

"Why didn't he?" Tom asked. "Why did he quit being an apprentice and become an archaeologist? Was it because Grandmom told him the truth about the rose?" He wondered if it had been too much for his father. Perhaps that was why his grandmother had resisted telling Tom for so long.

"Only he and your grandmother knew," Mr. Hu said, and tried to change the topic by waving a hand at an ornate building with pillars and a curved roof. Even though his claws were disguised as fingers, the nails were long and sharp. "Now do you see that bank over there? It used to be the telephone exchange." He hesitated. "Am I boring you?"

He was, but Tom was almost grateful for the change in topic. "No, go on." As the boy listened to the tiger, he felt as if he was falling under Chinatown's spell. Somewhere someone was blowing on a reed pipe, the mournful notes floating up the narrow alley to the strip of starlit sky overhead.

Mah-jong tiles clacked rhythmically like tiny drums.

He wasn't sure when the asphalt had given way to cobblestone and only noticed the change when he almost slipped on the bumpy surface. However, the tiger caught him by the collar. "Steady on, Master Thomas. The way to Goblin Square is not for the clumsy."

"Humans aren't as sure on their feet," Tom said, pulling free. As he straightened his collar, he glanced up at the streetlamp. Instead of being electric, it was a jet of gas. Finally they came to the mouth of an alley that was pitch-black. No light came from the buildings on either side. Mr. Hu plunged into it as confidently as if he were back in his own store.

"I can't see," Tom complained.

Annoyed, Mr. Hu guided Tom's hand to his coat. "Then hold on to me."

Gripping the hem of the tiger's jacket, Tom walked side by side with him into the alley. In the darkness, all he saw were the tiger's eyes, glowing a bright amber, and he gripped the tiger's coat tighter, afraid that if he lost Mr. Hu, he would never find his way out again.

"Ah, here we are," Mr. Hu said, and halted.

"What are we going to do now?" Tom asked, squinting hard at the darkness.

"Continue our stroll as soon as the moon rises, of course," Mr. Hu said, as if it should have been obvious.

"I knew it," Tom groaned. "You can't see either so you need the moonlight."

"Nothing of the sort," Mr. Hu said, annoyed. "Only the moon will open the road."

Tom saw the first silvery light tinge the rooftops overhead and then spill down the brick walls. And then a strange thing happened—the bricks began to glow. Tom thought he could see every detail of the bricks' surface and the mortar between, from the chips to the edges.

Suddenly where a wall had been was now a narrow street. And though he had not been aware of them before, he became aware of others waiting in the alley. Some had baskets, others even towed little handcarts. They all surged forward.

"Stay with me, Master Thomas," Mr. Hu said. Tom tightened his grasp upon the tiger's coat as Mr. Hu joined the crowd.

After a short while the cobblestones gave way to dirt, which made walking easier, and the brick walls on either side began to be walls of decorated wood and stone. Sometimes Tom saw bats, sometimes elephants, but there were many more strange creatures on the walls. With a shudder, he wondered if any of them were like the monsters that had attacked his grandmother.

Finally they came to a tall archway with columns carved with weird beings. Since Mr. Hu did not give them a glance, Tom assumed they were not monsters. Perhaps they were even the goblins that gave the square its name. Past the arch, they entered a large square surrounded on all sides by buildings like nothing Tom had ever seen. One was topped by a golden dome decorated with winged creatures. Another seemed to be carved all of ivory so that you could see inside to the rooms. It looked like a house of lace.

At first Tom thought the streetlamps were gaslit, but when he looked closer, he saw that there were flames inside that fluttered around inside the lamp like butterflies. "Are they alive?"

"Yes, they're fire sprites," Mr. Hu said, barely glancing up at them. "You feed them grass and straw three times a day, but their care can be quite complicated, so don't even think of keeping one for a pet."

In the square the crowd began to fan out, and Tom saw that only some of the travelers were humans. There were some with short hair and modern clothes. But many more had their hair done up in top knots or braids, and they seemed to be of every race. A man in a kilt walked by, his pale skin covered with tattoos, his blond hair in a heavy queue. He dipped his head respectfully to Mr. Hu, who nodded back.

Other customers were furred, others scaled, and Tom thought he saw a few beetlelike legs under robes scuttling across the square.

The various creatures quickly began to set up stalls around the edges of the square—not without a little bickering over choice spots. Some of the stalls looked as if they had been thrown together out of pieces of old crates and cardboard. But others were of hammered gold and silver with mother-of-pearl inlay and could have been in a museum.

"Ba-a-a," an animal bleated.

Tom turned and stared in amazement at a huge glass tank in which a sheep swam. When it baaed again, bubbles popped at the surface. Though its head was underwater, it seemed quite comfortable as it went back and forth from one end of the tank to the other, turning when its head butted against the glass.

"And what's that?" Tom asked, pointing at the strange creature.

Mr. Hu put a hand on Tom's hand and quickly pushed it down. "At Goblin Square it's considered rude to point with one finger, Master Thomas. If you must indicate something, do this," and he waved his entire hand. "That happens to be a water sheep from the Nine Brilliant Mountains. Their fleece repels water. My own suit is spun from their wool so I never have to worry about rain. And it never wrinkles so I never have to have it pressed."

"And it's high time you bought another suit," a voice said. "The one you're wearing went out of style fifty years ago."

Tom had been expecting Mr. Hu's friend to be another tiger or a human, so he was surprised to see a dragon. She was curled up like a cat next to a stall made out of giant bones.

She wasn't very large—about the same size as Mr. Hu; her body was thin as whipcord, and her daggerlike claws looked even deadlier than the tiger's. The scoring and dents in her scales testified to many battles.

When she stirred, he could see the powerful muscles ripple beneath the hide of her slender legs and torso, yet she didn't look nearly as strong or deadly as the dragons always did in books.

What he had not expected was how beautiful a dragon could be. Her scarred scales were black as chips of night, and in the light falling from the stall's fire sprite lanterns, the edges gleamed iridescent, so that the dragon seemed a creature carved out of obsidian caught in a rainbow net.

Mr. Hu strolled over to her. "My, my, Mistral, how the mighty Harmatannids have fallen—but you'll make a fine doorstop for someone."

The dragon lifted her head with a playful growl. "I'll have you know that I am a bodyguard to a very wealthy and important merchant. I have never been an article of furniture for anyone."

"From the filth on the stall, I doubt that," Mr. Hu grunted, "but I suppose it makes you feel better to think that."

A slender, furry creature with large black eyes the size of saucers popped up from behind a display of spices. "Bhima at your service," he said, bobbing his head up and down like a toy as he kept bowing. "And since you're a friend of Mistral's, I'll give you a good discount."

Mistral lay her head back down. "Don't bother, Bhima.

He came to see me."

"Oh," Bhima said, disappointed, and disappeared back behind the counter. From the clink of the jars, Tom supposed the merchant was still unpacking his stock.

Mr. Hu squatted down beside the dragon. "I would think you'd be tired of guarding pots by now."

"It pays good," Mistral said, closing her eyes, "and I get to sightsee quite a bit."

"We have more than pots—though we have the finest if you need them. But I really stock the Wonders of the World," Bhima boasted, waving a paw at the banner over his stall, which announced to everyone that Bhima's Emporium was where all the kings and queens of the globe came for their desires; there were even helpful illustrations for those who could not read.

"I have a job for you," Mr. Hu coaxed. "Something more worthy of the talents of a descendant of Harmattan, the son of Calambac."

The dragon yawned. "Like what?"

Mr. Hu lowered his voice. "I can't go into details now. I need the bold warrior who once faced the king of all dragons and called him a fool."

"I never said that," Mistral said, shifting her head.

The tiger folded his arms. "So rumor claims."

"I called him a lazy clown," Mistral corrected Mr. Hu.

"And so I need that same honorable dragon," the tiger coaxed.

"That dragon is dead," Mistral mumbled. "For too long she has had to eat the rice of strangers." Mistral finally opened one eye to stare at the tiger. "It's strictly cash in advance now."

"This would have to be out of friendship," Mr. Hu said.

"I have no friends," Mistral snorted. "The lives of non-dragons are too short compared to mine so it's pointless to cultivate them. And all dragons have turned their backs on me."

"And yet you and I were close at one time," Mr. Hu said.

Mistral frowned. "Another error in a life of errors. Find someone else."

"I thought dragons were supposed to be brave and noble," Tom said indignantly, "not greedy slugs."

"This hatchling needs to be taught some manners." Mistral turned her open eye toward the boy. "Whoever he is."

"This is Mistress Lee's grandson," Mr. Hu said softly. "The Ghost Cart carried her away this afternoon."

Instantly the dragon's manner changed. Her eyes were both open as she raised her head again. "I saw it in the distance, but I didn't know it was for her." She bowed her head respectfully. "Your grandmother was a great and generous woman. Once I was so seriously wounded that I thought the Ghost Cart would come for me, but she nursed me back to health."

"Thanks," Tom said, beginning to think better of the dragon.

"We need you," Mr. Hu said.

Mistral glanced at Bhima and then dragged a claw over a cobblestone. "But this job is comfortable even if we do travel around the world."

"Did Mistress Lee ever worry about her comfort?" Mr. Hu asked.

Mistral arched her elegant neck so she could press her face against Mr. Hu's. "You are shameless."

"Absolutely," Mr. Hu agreed. "I can't protect her grandson on my own."

"Is he at peril or," Mistral asked meaningfully, "is something else?"

"What do you think?" Mr. Hu asked. "But your ancestress Longwhistle would be proud for you to undertake this mission."

"Don't talk about ancestors," Mistral said bitterly. "I have none. My family disowned me just so they could protect their own comfort and privileges."

"Even if you have no debt to your family, you still owe Mistress Lee," the tiger reminded her.

Mistral sighed. "You're shameless, but your point is unfortunately well taken. She was a jewel among humans. I'm sure she was a dragon in another life." Mistral said it as if that were the highest form of compliment.

"Yes, she was a fine person." Mr. Hu beamed.

"No, no, no, you cannot steal my bodyguard." Bhima leaped down from the counter onto the dragon's back.

Scrambling up, he wrapped tiny black paws around the dragon's neck and began to wail and weep. "She is like a daughter to me."

"Bhima, I'll find someone to take my place," Mistral promised.

As Bhima clung to her neck, he asked slyly, "I don't have to pay you for the three days you worked this week?"

When the dragon hesitated, the tiger reminded her, "This is for Mistress Lee, who helped you when every hand and paw were turned against you."

Mistral winced. "Hu, you are worse than shameless." With a heavy sigh Mistral nodded her head to her present employer. "No, you don't have to pay me."

Bhima's sorrow vanished completely as he hopped nimbly back up to his counter. "The replacement must be reliable."

"Yes, yes," Mistral said, getting up. "I'll start looking around right now."

"You're so good at faking feelings, you should have been an actor," Tom told the merchant.

"Acting is piffle-paffle," Bhima said with a modest wave of his paw. "Bargaining is everything."

"Find that replacement soon," Mr. Hu urged.

As they wandered down the aisle, Tom asked, "Can you trust her? She seems a little greedy."

Mr. Hu stopped by a stall made out of old hides. "Don't be so quick to judge Mistral. If she first thinks of herself, it's because her life as an outlaw has taught her that. The only one who was kind to her was Mistress Lee. She saw Mistral's true heart when no one else did, but that was ever your grandmother's way with people—from dragons to humans and at least one tiger."

Tom glanced back over his shoulder at the dragon, who had coiled up on the ground again like a jeweled black rope. "She's beautiful though."

"It's what a poet once called a terrible beauty," Mr. Hu said, following his gaze. "She's like a sword covered with gems, lovely to look at but deadly."

"And who is Longwhistle?" Tom asked.

"A dragon who created the Feather Grotto and the Fire Gardens, among other wonders of the dragon kingdom," Mr. Hu said, selecting a toothbrush. "Ah, warthog bristles." He nodded to Tom. "They'll clean your fangs best."

Tom tried to ask more questions, but Mr. Hu insisted on concentrating on the task at hand: getting the necessities for a human cub. However, since the elderly tiger didn't have a clue as to what those were, he left it to Tom to buy such things as clothes and underwear—which they could have done at a regular department store.

But the dandyish tiger would not have been able to indulge his own tastes in a human establishment, because there would have been no cravats of silk woven by dragons in the Underwater Kingdom. Nor would there have been books written by ghost sages, the pages of which were as light as tissue and seemed to float when you read them and the words of which appeared and disappeared with a breath.

They did not stop shopping until Tom had almost as much as he could carry. The tiger would have left then, but Mistral had never been far from Tom's mind and he felt he ought to buy the dragon a gift to make up for being so critical of her. He couldn't take back his first words. "What do dragons eat anyway?"

"Little boys," Mr. Hu said, grinning wickedly.

The thought of the dragon's great fangs and claws made Tom want to take to his heels, but he forced himself to stay put. "Besides that." He nodded to the square. "Is there something else she'd like?"

Mr. Hu rocked up and down on his heels. "Harumph, you're being awfully free with my money."

Tom looked warily at the tiger, who seemed so sensitive about his authority. Swallowing, he risked saying, "We never had many visitors, but my grandmother always tried to make them feel welcome." Even if few of them had ever come back. "If Mistral's going to visit you, you ought to have something. I'll use my own money if I have to. Do they take American cash?"

"They take anything of value." The tiger squirmed a moment and then cleared his throat. "Well, I can think of one thing Mistral would like."

He led Tom over to a little bakery cart that sold fish-shaped cakes filled with a sweet sea slug paste. Though Mr.

Hu would have bought them, Tom insisted on doing it. Of course, the bag of cakes was added to Tom's load as well.

On the way back to the store, Mr. Hu bought the late edition of the newspaper. There on the front page was a picture of a pit where Mistress Lee's house had once stood.

The article said that there were few clues in the burnt rubble to the cause of the explosion, but the authorities seemed inclined to blame it on a gas pipe. They were waiting for the debris to cool before they sifted through it; but from the photo Tom doubted they would find his grandmother's remains. They would think both he and his grandmother had died.

Tom fought back his tears and looked around him at the busy street. A distracted woman hurried by, her hands full of plastic bags stuffed with groceries. A man passed by pushing along a rack of blouses. "Look at them. No idea of monsters. I wish we could have told the police. Everyone used to call her a weirdo—someone should know how brave she was."

"A Guardian's battles are solitary ones and fought in the shadows. A very few must protect the many, and with no thanks for their efforts," Mr. Hu said, but he picked up his pace as if he were in a hurry now to reach the store.

Once inside, he slapped a charm upon the front door. "There, we should be safe now."

Tom was still skeptical after seeing how his grandmother's wards had been destroyed. "Will that keep the monsters out?" He tried the door, but it acted as if it was glued shut.

Mr. Hu saw how sad and anxious his apprentice looked and tried to comfort him. "Have no fear, Master Thomas. The thieves will find this a fortress against them."

The tiger inspected the rest of the wards in front and then went into the rear apartment to check the ones there. Tom felt exposed in the store on his own and, with a shiver, he followed the tiger.

When the tiger had double- and triple-checked all his wards, they held their own memorial for Tom's grandmother. Mr. Hu wrote her name in Chinese on a tablet and set it up on a small table with tiny cups of sand. Into these he thrust burning sticks of incense, and in a bowl he burned shiny paper money and paper servants and even a paper house—all of which he had purchased at Goblin Square.

When the tiger cried, he muttered, "I don't know what they're putting in the incense nowadays. That smoke irritates my eyes."

Tom stared at the Guardian. There were times when he seemed like a wild beast, and yet there were other times, like now, when he seemed quite human. "Mine too," he said.

Giving one last swipe to his eyes with the back of his hand, Mr. Hu said, "Well, it's been a hard day. I could use some sleep, so let's turn in. You can have my bed tonight. Then we'll sort out something for you tomorrow."

Mr. Hu's bed was in a room small enough to be a closet.

The bed was only a cot. Most of the room was taken up by a bureau carved with strange flowers and trees and birds. There was barely enough space for both the tiger and boy to squeeze in. The tiger cleared off the clutter of statues and books.

Tom wasn't frightened at first until the tiger turned off the light and left the room. Suddenly the black bulk of the furniture loomed over him like a monster. And the old boards of the store creaked to one another in squeaky complaints—probably about the inconsiderate boy pounding around all day.

As he lay in the dark, he remembered the monsters' claws again. "Now would be a great time to wake up."

He closed his eyes, telling himself that he was really at his grandmother's. And when he opened his eyes, he would go into the kitchen and find her making hot cocoa with little marshmallows for him.

But when he opened his eyes, he was still in the strange room with an even stranger tiger outside.

"It's time to quit dreaming," he said, and pinched himself very hard. But he remained in the room, and now his forearm hurt.

The worst of it all was that his grandmother was really dead. He'd never felt more alone. And he'd never felt more lost. She'd been the one person who really loved him. And yet he had abandoned her when she had needed him. He'd been absolutely worthless to her when it really counted. The shame was so intense, he ached inside.

When he heard a thump outside, he slipped out of bed and peeked out the door.

Bright amber eyes glowed in the darkness. "Go to sleep, Master Thomas," Mr. Hu said.

But Tom groped by the doorway until he turned on the bedroom light. "Can't you sleep either?"

Enough light fell into the next room to show him the tiger sitting in a chair before the rose. He had taken off his suit and gotten comfortable in a Princeton sweatshirt and sweatpants and had taken his true shape again. Then, as Tom stared harder, he saw that Mr. Hu's cheeks glistened.

Hurriedly the tiger raised a paw to shield his face from view. "I'm keeping watch, so don't worry. Go back to bed."

Tom was curious. He padded across the cold floorboards until he was right by the tiger.

Embarrassed, Mr. Hu turned his head. "I told you to sleep, Master Thomas."

Tom circled the chair so he could see the tiger's face. "You're crying again."

Mr. Hu wiped at his face, but the tears kept wetting his skin. "There never will be anyone like Mistress Lee. She was the only one I ever loved. And I could not save her."

Seeing the powerful tiger weep, Tom felt his own eyes sting. "Me too." And he began to cry as well.

"I only hope you and I can do half as well as she did." Mr. Hu hung his head and his great body shook.

The tiger looked so sad that Tom put his arm around Mr. Hu's shoulders. "You'll do okay," Tom assured him. "She chose you, didn't she?" Tom was startled when the tiger laid his head on Tom's chest. The weight nearly knocked the boy down.

Suddenly Mr. Hu straightened. "This is a terrible way to begin my Guardianship—bawling like a calf." He brushed his sleeve over his face. "I swear I will punish whoever attacked her."

"Grandmom always said it was okay to cry," Tom said, wiping at his own eyes.

Mr. Hu stared at him uncomfortably and then looked down at his toes. "Master Thomas, I've always been too busy fighting to have a family, so I confess I don't know much about cubs, and I never expected to have one underpaw." Tom looked up again and the tiger's great amber eyes seemed to grow larger and larger until the boy thought he would fall into them. The tiger gave a growl so deep it seemed to vibrate in Tom's own chest. "But Mistress Lee trusted you to me, as well as the rose. And I swear that as long as I draw breath, you will not come to harm."

Tom could almost hear Grandmom whispering to him that, as terrifying as the tiger could be, Mr. Hu would slash his own throat before he would ever hurt her grandson. Tom stared at Mr. Hu for a long time. The tiger had loved Tom's grandmother as much as he did, so he couldn't be all that bad, and he even seemed to be trying to extend that love to the grandson of his beloved mistress.

Wild or tame, maybe it was good to have Mr. Hu on his side. "Thank you," he said.

When Tom went back to bed, he left the door open so he could see the tiger's eyes glow in the darkness, watching for monsters. And knowing that the Guardian was keeping watch over him as vigilantly and tenderly as over his precious rose, the boy forgot to be sad and afraid and finally fell asleep.

CHAPTER SIX

Loo is a creature with
a blue face and red hair and clothes.
He has fangs and three eyes.
He uses an umbrella to spread illness.
—Chinese tradition

All the next morning, Mr. Hu paced back and forth in the store, weaving a tortuous path in and out of the collected antiques. "Blast. Where is Mistral? Until she comes, all I can do is wait here like prey."

Tom didn't particularly care for the Guardian's choice of words. It made him think of some goat set out as bait. "You're used to doing the hunting?"

Mr. Hu smiled. "I was always a better hunter than I was an apprentice." Having seen his true shape, Tom wouldn't want to have the tiger tracking him.

As he watched Mr. Hu prowl restlessly, Tom couldn't help thinking that the Guardian might look human but inside he was still a tiger. "Did you really expect to retire and sell antiques?"

Mr. Hu paused. "When I was in the midst of battles, a peaceful life as a shopkeeper seemed like such a remote, happy dream." The tiger chuckled deeply in his throat. "Be careful what you wish for, Master Thomas."

The tiger spun around and Tom gave a jump when someone rattled the doorknob and then knocked at the glass.

"Mr. H?" Sidney called. "Let me in."

When Tom turned, he saw the small, round, yellow rat hopping up and down excitedly and rapping at the door as if he were trying to break inside.

"Blast that rat!" Mr. Hu snarled. "He probably wants to sell me some trash he found." He waved his hand at Sidney. "Whatever you've got, I'm not buying."

The rat kept right on knocking. "He never takes no for an answer, does he?" Tom asked.

"It's not part of his vocabulary," Mr. Hu said, stalking to the door, "and unfortunately neither is 'go away.'" Taking off the charm and unlocking the door, Mr. Hu yanked it open. "I don't want anything, Sidney!"

"Oh, you'll want this." The agile rat slipped between the tiger's legs and inside the store. "I heard this guy nosing around last night, asking about the boy." Unfortunately Sidney could not hold a conversation without inspecting every item in reach of his paws. "Ooo, that's nice."

Slamming the door shut again, Mr. Hu liberated a porcelain bowl from the rat's paws. "Careful, that's fragile." When he had safely set it out of Sidney's reach, Mr. Hu went on, "Did you recognize him?"

"Sorry, Mr. H. Never seen him before and nobody else has either." Sidney picked up a small statue. "He was as ugly as a lizard can get. So I followed him for a while, but I lost his trail."

"You don't have a tiger's stalking skills." Mr. Hu's eyes brightened and his foot began to tap with so much excitement that he did not notice the danger to the statue that the rat was tossing back and forth from paw to paw. "Could you take me to the spot where you last saw him?"

"Sure thing, Mr. H." Sidney was so busy nodding his head that the statue slipped through his paws. "Morning," he said to Tom as the boy caught it and placed it on a high shelf.

Mr. Hu glanced in the direction of the street as if he longed to be on the hunt again and then sighed. "I have to wait here until Mistral comes to watch the store."

Sidney shook his head. "No good, Mr. H.; the trail will get cold. We've got to leave now."

Mr. Hu paced in and around the antiques. Finally he stopped, nodding his head firmly. "We mustn't waste this opportunity. If we can track him to his lair, it's worth the risk."

Tom was also finding the store a little cramped. "It'll be good to get outside."

To the boy's surprise, the Guardian said, "I'm sorry, Master Thomas. The rose is safer here and someone must remain in the store to place the charm back upon the door after I depart. It's already been enchanted so you won't need any more spells. You just have to put it on the glass. It's a task that's very easy but just as important as tracking our enemies."

Tom knew when an adult was trying to fool him. "You mean I'm stuck here?"

"I'm afraid so," the tiger said, scratching his cheek in embarrassment.

Tom looked around the dusty old shop in dismay. "How long will you be gone?"

"It could be awhile." Mr. Hu shrugged. "On my way back, I should also see if that blasted dragon's had any luck finding a replacement." He handed Tom the charm. "Tape this on the door after we leave. Do not let Mistral in. She'll understand when you explain the situation. And even if you see someone who looks like me, do not remove it until you hear me knock. Like so." He rapped his paw on the door twice and then twice more.

Disappointed, Tom scolded himself. He had been stupid to believe Mr. Hu's talk about the bond between the Guardian and his apprentice. He was no different from the school counselors who had talked about trust but never meant it. As soon as Tom got in trouble, they did a report with a lot of fancy words and turned him over to someone else.

The thing that hurt the most was that he'd let himself be fooled again. At least none of the school counselors had abandoned Tom to face monsters on his own as the Guardian was doing.

Well, it was time he started to think about himself first.

"I quit," Tom said.

Mr. Hu's head jerked up in disbelief. "You what?"

Tom set his jaw defiantly. "I don't want to be your apprentice anymore. What kind of Guardian would expect me to deal with monsters by myself? Grandmom never would have."

Sidney stared at the tiger in awe. "You're the Guardian now. Then that means—"

"Yes, Sidney," Mr. Hu said, and turned back to the boy. "Master Thomas, you have plenty of protection." He waved the charm in his hand. "How can you turn your back on everything your grandmother fought for? If Mistress Lee were alive, she'd be ashamed of you for talking about quitting."

Tom felt a twinge inside at that accusation but he held his ground. "I only learned the Lore to please my grandmother. And I wouldn't have done that if I knew just how bad the monsters would be."

Mr. Hu's amber eyes stared at him in puzzlement. "I will never understand human cubs. They are so willful." He slapped his sides in frustration. "Well, do this much for your grandmother's sake: Stay here until I return. I will find someone else." Again he thrust the charm at the boy.

Tom hesitated, but he guessed he owed his grandmother that much. "Okay, but as soon as you get back, I'm out of here," Tom grumbled as he finally took it.

Mr. Hu looked worried. "Where will you go, Master Thomas?"

Tom held the charm against his chest. "I don't know.

I guess some foster home if I have to."

Mr. Hu blinked, hurt. "I'm sorry you feel that way. I promised your grandmother that I would protect you, so I will see what I can do to carry out your wishes." When Mr. Hu had stepped outside with Sidney, he turned and watched Tom as he pasted the charm to the glass of the front door. Satisfied that the store was secure, he loped off, apparently eager to be on the hunt again and away from the irresponsible human cub.

Tom watched the tiger disappear and then turned. Suddenly the strange shop seemed very large, and every creak and groan of the old building made Tom look around. The newspaper article had brought back the horror of yesterday afternoon, and he could imagine something hiding in the many shadows of the cluttered shop.

Feeling betrayed, lonely, and frightened, Tom found himself drifting into the rear apartment to the memorial. Even though he had seen the smoke with his own eyes, it still didn't seem possible that his grandmother was dead. He put out a fresh cup of tea before the tablet and added one of the star-shaped fruits that Mr. Hu had also bought last night in Goblin Square.

"I'm sorry, Grandmom," he whispered to the tablet as he sat down. "But I'm scared. I know you wouldn't want me to do something I didn't want to." Even so, he couldn't help feeling that he was letting his grandmother down. As he sat, miserable and alone, he heard a rapping on the door.

Cautiously, he peeked from the apartment toward the front door. A girl about his age was standing there.

"Help. Please help me," she begged in Chinese.

Tom stared at her because the girl, who was about his age, did not look Asian. She was short and slender, dressed in a white sweater, jeans, and sneakers. Her narrow chin and wide cheekbones gave her a foxish look. Her fluffy silvery hair, which she had gathered up on either side of her head, swung like wings as she banged at the door.

"Please. Something's following me," she pleaded frantically.

She looked so frightened that he began to feel sorry for her. After all, he reasoned, he shouldn't be suspicious just because she didn't look like the others in Chinatown. Neither did he. *"I call police,"* he said in his own limited Chinese. What he'd learned, he'd picked up from his grandmother.

"They won't come in time," the girl said, switching to English. In her desperation, she tried the doorknob. "Please let me in."

But the Guardian's orders had been so clear that Tom still hesitated. "I can't."

"Please, please." The girl was banging on the door frantically. "They'll get me."

He thought again of the monsters on the roof. He wouldn't want to leave anyone at their mercy, and she seemed harmless enough. Mr. Hu had warned him not to open the door, but he wouldn't want an innocent person to suffer. And how could Tom stay in safety and watch the monster attack her?

"Hurry." The girl glanced down the street. "They're coming."

He was sure his grandmother would not have left the girl to her fate. Quickly Tom made his way to the front door, but even so, despite the girl's pleas, he peered out, looking for monsters. When he didn't see any in view, he began to peel back the charm.

"Okay, I'm going to unlock the door but step inside quick. What's your name?"

The girl was so stunned he was listening to her entreaty that it took her a moment to answer. "Räv."

Once the charm was removed, the door opened easily. "Hurry. Get in," Tom urged.

Instead of seeking refuge Räv stood there, confused. "Why are you doing this?"

"It's what you wanted, isn't it?" Tom demanded. "I couldn't leave anyone to a monster." He motioned her into the shop.

Even now, Räv hesitated on the threshold as she gazed at him, puzzled. "Thank you. It's . . . kind of you." She lingered on the word as if the concept was strange to her.

That's the last word his teachers and schoolmates would have used for him. "It's not kindness," Tom said as he swung the door back. "It's just that I know how I'd feel in your shoes."

"Maybe that's what real kindness is," Räv said almost

guiltily. As she finally entered the store, her arm happened to brush his and she stepped back with a cry.

"What's wrong?" Tom asked in alarm, glancing at his arm.

"It must be static electricity." Räv rubbed her fingers.

The next instant a strange creature suddenly dropped down onto the sidewalk from his perch on the storefront above the window. His face was bright blue but his eyebrows and hair were the same scarlet as his suit with the long tails—as if he had just come from a nightclub.

Set at a rakish angle on his head was a top hat, also of red, and he leaned on a purple Chinese umbrella of oiled paper. He might have been the picture of a gentleman from a high-fashion magazine except for the long, sharp teeth that protruded from the corners of his mouth and the three eyes that stared in triumph at Tom.

Pointing the umbrella at the boy, the creature began to open it. Tom saw words written on it in a strange script mixed in with pictures of skulls and monsters.

"Down!" Räv impulsively threw herself against him so hard that the both of them fell backward. With a teeth-jarring crack, Tom's head hit a small cabinet. And then the world was dark.

"Hu, old boy, you've shaved," a voice drawled. "And you've also shrunk."

Tom opened his eyes to see another stranger, a short

man, squatting down beside him. His hair was a tawny yellow, almost like a lion's. On his head flopped a cap of silk, and he was wearing a white suit over a compact, powerful body. In his eyes was a mischievous spark that seemed to invite everyone to have fun. The girl Räv was gone.

Tom forgot to be afraid. He finally had a chance at one of the thieves who had been attacking them. His hand groped blindly for something and he found a stick. "Take that!" When he whipped the stick toward the stranger's head, he saw it was really a broken chair leg.

Though he swung as hard as he could, the stranger nimbly jumped to a table, scattering plates and vases on the floor with a crash. "Next time swing from the hips and not the shoulders, Hu."

"Get out of here," Tom yelled. He felt dizzy as he aimed wildly at the man again.

The nimble stranger did a graceful back flip that took him through the door into the apartment behind the store. "And your wrists should be more flexible."

Hoping against hope, Tom stumbled toward the rear apartment. Broken bits of porcelain and glass crunched under his shoes. The glass case lay on the floor. The rose was gone! He hunted for the stranger and found him sitting on top of a set of shelves between a couple of demon masks. "You'll be sorry if you don't give it back."

The stranger cupped his chin in his hands. "I'm glad to see you still have the same bad temper."

"I warned you." Tom threw the chair leg.

The stranger ducked easily. "But your aim is worse than usual."

"Get down here and fight!" Tom snatched a broom from a corner and started to poke it up at the stranger.

The stranger yawned as he batted it away with a hand. "This is the address Hu sent me and he said he'd be here, but the Hu I know would never be caught dead in those clothes. So I guess you can't be him in disguise."

"Give it back," Tom shouted, continuing to thrust at the stranger.

"I would if I knew what it was you wanted," the stranger said, catching the broom handle easily in his hand. "And it would help to know who you are."

"I'm Mr. Hu's apprentice. At least for a while," Tom said. "My name's Tom Lee."

The stranger jabbed a finger at Tom. "Ha! If you were Hu's apprentice, he would have told you I was coming. For I am," the stranger declared proudly, "the Great Sage Equal to Heaven. Mr. Hu sent for me."

"That's an awful big title," Tom sniffed, "for such a small person."

The Great Sage transformed into a golden ape; but unlike Mr. Hu, his clothes also changed. Now he was wearing a floppy silken cap and gray robes.

Puffing out his chest, he proudly announced, "I am the Master of the Seventy-Two Transformations, the rider of clouds—"

"—And the biggest liar and thief in the Seven Seas,"

Mistral's voice said. "I don't know what's going on, but you have to be behind it. I came just in time."

Mistral must have finally found her replacement, and none too soon. Tom whirled around expecting to see the dragon, but instead he saw a woman in a fancy lamé suit that shimmered like a rainbow. The next moment she had launched herself into the air, transforming as she leaped, reaching out hands that became scaled paws with sharp claws in the blink of an eye. Even her suit changed back into shiny black scales.

Tom barely got out of the way in time; but the Great Sage somersaulted off the shelves, landing upon the dragon's back. "Mistral! I haven't seen you in ages."

The dragon crashed to the floor, writhing about as she tried to toss the ape from her back. "Get off me, you furry fleabag." What little furniture hadn't been smashed before was turned into splinters now.

If the dragon had a strange, deadly beauty, then so did the golden ape. You just didn't realize it, Tom thought, until you saw him move. Then he was like a furry lightning bolt that flashed through the air. The Sage could not only hold his own against a dragon but he had fun doing it.

Corkscrewing her body across the floor, the dragon finally threw the Great Sage off. As he landed on the floor, she coiled her body around him and pointed deadly claws at his throat. "You'll pay for your crimes."

"I've missed you too," the ape said amiably.

Mistral looked at Tom. "What's this furbag done?"

"There's a . . . a coral rose is missing." Tom pointed to the space on the table where it had been. "But I don't think the Great Sage took it. He says Mr. Hu called him too."

The dragon glared at the ape. "First of all, his name is Monkey—no matter what grand airs he tries to give himself. And you don't know how nimble a thief he is. He stole a magical staff right out of the Dragon King's palace."

"The staff was just gathering dust," Monkey argued. "What good's magic if you don't use it?"

"Please," Tom said. He put his hands on the dragon's coils. The scales felt dry, even pleasant. "You mustn't fight. Mr. Hu called you both. I'm sure he wanted you to help protect the rose." Tom felt a sinking feeling. "But it's already gone."

"We'll help you get the rose back." But Monkey could not resist mischief for long. Turning, he patted the dragon's cheek. "Won't we, old friend?"

The dragon snapped her head back out of reach of his paw. "We are not nor will we ever be friends." But she loosened her coils and glanced at Tom. "Is the rose what I think it is?"

"Yes," Tom confessed.

Monkey glanced at the dragon. "Mistress Lee had the rose when last I heard."

"She's dead," Tom said, feeling the ache inside.

"I'm sorry." Monkey took off his cap. "She'll be missed."

The enormity of the rose's loss was just starting to sink in. Tom felt as if someone had snatched away the floor, and he leaned against a table. Not only had he run away when his grandmother was in trouble, but now he had lost the very thing for which she had given her life. "The thief wrecked everything. He didn't even leave your cakes alone." He held up one of the pungent pieces from the broken bakery cart bag.

"You got them for me?" Mistral asked. With obvious delight, she plucked one of the smelly bits from Tom's palm. "But these are my favorites. How did you know?"

"I asked Mr. Hu," Tom said. He tried to find a clean piece, but there weren't any.

"But why?" Mistral said. "You said I was greedy."

"You're still a guest." Tom shrugged.

Mistral slowly smiled. "You're much like your grandmother, Mistress Lee."

Knowing how highly the dragon regarded his grandmother, Tom felt bad when he looked at the broken cakes. "I wanted to have something for you when you came to visit—just like she would have. But now the cakes are all dirty."

"In my wanderings, I've found that dirt adds spice to some things." And she tossed the bit into her mouth and chewed, savoring the flavor.

"I hope you don't get sick," Tom said anxiously as he

handed the other fragments to the dragon.

"Old iron gut?" Monkey said as he slouched against a wall. "Not a chance. Dragons are even better gluttons than they are braggarts."

Eagerly Mistral reached beyond Tom to snatch up the bag. "When every hand and paw were raised against me and I first began wandering the land, your grandmother was kind to me. I've treasured her memory in all my troubles. And you are as kind as she was."

Tom watched as the dragon greedily finished off the rest of the cakes. His grandmother would definitely have been pleased.

"Are you all right, boy?" Monkey asked. "There's blood on your face."

Sure enough when Tom put a hand to his forehead, he felt a wetness. "I can feel a bump but not a cut."

Monkey pointed to the storefront. "There are some drops of blood, but I guess not yours."

"The blood must be Räv's," Tom said, finally remembering the girl. "There was some kind of monster chasing her. The monster must have gotten her as well." He wiped his sleeve over the bump.

"What's going on?" Mr. Hu roared from the store. "There's blood on the floor! Master Thomas, are you all right?"

Tom turned in surprise. Perhaps the Guardian really did care about him after all.

"I'm okay," Tom called to him.

"Thank heaven for that," Mr. Hu said fervently as he came to the doorway into the rear apartment.

Sidney peered from around the tiger's legs and let out a whistle. "Geez, time to do some spring cleaning, Mr. H." He started to dig around in his fur. "I got a nice assortment of dustpans and whisk brooms in here somewhere."

"The rose!" The tiger hunched as fur, claws, and fangs appeared again; he sprang into the room, his hind paws crunching on the broken bits of tablet. He stood for a moment staring down at it in horror. "Whoever did this will pay!"

Raising a paw, he unsheathed his claws and his tail began to whip back and forth like a snake. He fell on all fours, crouching, ears flat and tight against his skull, once again the jungle animal Tom had seen in the battle with the monsters on his grandmother's roof.

The boy shrank back, afraid, but the dragon took the transformation calmly enough as she said, "You can be sure of that."

With a growl, Mr. Hu spun around. "I would have sworn my wards would hold." Suddenly he caught sight of Tom and he forced himself to straighten up. "What happened to the door, Master Thomas?"

Tom wanted to crawl into the nearest hole, but he thought of what his grandmother had done when the monsters had come and instead forced himself to face the tiger.

"There was this girl being chased by a monster. I'm sorry. I had to take the charm from the door," Tom said, and told the tiger briefly what had happened. Then he waited for the tiger to explode.

Instead, Mr. Hu heaved a deep sigh. "I see. The thief used the threat against the girl to make you open the door—but you did right. I don't see that you had any choice. You could not stand by and let an innocent person suffer." To Tom's surprise, Mr. Hu patted him approvingly on the shoulder. "Do you remember what this thief looked like?"

When Tom had finished describing the monster, Mr. Hu glanced at Mistral. "It sounds like Loo."

"Especially the umbrella." The dragon nodded, and glanced at the boy. "It's a good thing you avoided it. When it's opened, it sends out fumes full of such foul diseases that you would die in an instant."

"And Loo serves Vatten," Monkey said.

"Worse and worse," Mistral said, shaking her head.

"Who's Vatten?" Tom asked.

"When he was known as the Storm Sentry, he was Kung Kung's closest lieutenant," Mistral said somberly. "He's a master of shape-shifting who has never stopped seeking revenge for his master. When the rebellion was crushed, he fooled his pursuers into thinking he was dead. Over the centuries, he has adopted many names and forms. Vatten is his latest. He'll use the phoenix to force everyone to do what he wants. And what he wants is total chaos."

Monkey looked grim for once. "It could be the end of the world."

"Not 'could,'" Mistral said darkly. "It will be."

Sidney pounded one paw against another. "Well, we'll just have to get the rose back then."

Mr. Hu pounced, snatching the rat up by the scruff of his neck. "How much did they pay you to lead me away, Sidney?"

Kicking his hind paws uselessly in the air, the rat squealed desperately, "No, no, I'd never double-cross a partner."

"Until someone pays you more," the tiger growled, baring wicked-looking fangs.

"Mr. H," Sidney said, raising his bald pink tail indignantly, "I got my standards."

"And every one of them has the picture of Benjamin Franklin on it," Mr. Hu said, rubbing the claws of his free paw together as if he was holding money.

Sidney's tail dangled sadly in the air. "Mr. H," the rat said, grieved, "is that what you really think of me?"

"It's only a small part," Mr. Hu snapped. "And I don't have time to tell you all the rest." Mr. Hu jerked his head at Tom. "There's some cord over in that corner that I use for wrapping packages. Get it."

"What are you doing, Mr. H?" Sidney gasped as he began to wriggle frantically.

"Putting you away so you can't tell your master," Mr. Hu said.

Tom found the bundle of cord and brought it over to the tiger, who tied up the struggling rat like a parcel.

"Let me come with you," Sidney begged. "You need me."

"You've helped enough already," Mr. Hu declared. He deposited the rat inside the vault. "You should have enough air in there if you don't talk. We'll let you out—if your master lets us live."

"I can help you," Sidney squealed as Mr. Hu closed the vault door with a thud.

Sure that the rat could not hear them through the thick door, Mr. Hu told the others, "The spy that asked about Master Thomas left a trail that leads to a mansion by the sea. Perhaps that's where the thieves went also."

Monkey had taken a metal toothpick from behind his ear and was using it to scratch his cheek. "The spy was a diversion. Maybe their lair is too."

"Vatten's element is water, so he draws strength from it," Mistral said. "He'll be even more powerful close to the ocean."

"Even if it's not their lair, there are bound to be tracks and clues there," Monkey reasoned, "that would lead us to the thieves."

"Or to a trap," Mr. Hu said thoughtfully.

Monkey tucked the toothpick back behind his ear. "Well, if this is all we have, it's to their lair we'll go."

Raising a paw, Mistral swore, "The thieves will be sorry." Tom thought she had never looked more deadly and yet never more beautiful.

Tom started to think of all the terrible things that could

happen. So, although he was scared of monsters, he said shakily, "I want to go too."

Mr. Hu clasped his paws behind his back. "Master Thomas, you said you wanted to quit when I came back. What's changed your mind?"

After hearing how dangerous Loo could be, Tom would have liked nothing better than to leave, but he had to ask. "Was Loo the one who attacked Grandmom?"

"He would be powerful enough to have harmed the Guardian," Mr. Hu said.

"Then," Tom said after taking a deep breath, "I want to catch Loo and get my grandmom's rose and Räv back. Maybe they've hurt her."

Mr. Hu studied the boy but finally shook his head. "It's too dangerous for you to accompany us to face Loo. You're not ready."

"It'll be more dangerous if Loo keeps the rose," Tom argued.

"The boy is right," Mistral said. "Once the phoenix hatches, Vatten can use it to force everyone to do what he wants. There will be safety for none. His place is by your side."

Surprised and grateful, Tom looked at the dragon. Despite his harsh words at the Square, she was standing up for him.

"But he's barely begun his lessons," Mr. Hu argued.

"Dragons live such a long time that we know a bit more

about destiny than most creatures," Mistral said quietly. "I believe both your fates are tied together with the rose."

Mr. Hu thought about it a good long time before he finally nodded. "Very well."

When the magical creatures had each transformed into human shape, they left the store. Behind them, Tom could still hear the little rat squeaking from the vault.

"Shouldn't we give him some water at least?" Tom asked.

"He's got a better chance than we do." For once even Monkey looked serious. "But it's exciting times ahead, however you look at it."

CHAPTER SEVEN

"Why do we have to catch a bus again?" Tom asked Mr. Hu as they waited by the stop.

Mr. Hu arched a bushy eyebrow. "You may walk, if you want."

"Can't you work a spell or something that will take us wherever we're going?" Tom demanded. "Aren't we in a hurry?"

Mr. Hu tugged irritably at his goatee. "Those kind of spells exhaust the magician, and I must save all my strength for the coming battle."

"Well"—Tom glanced at Mistral—"maybe we could hitch a ride on someone's back."

"I'm not running a taxi service," Mistral snapped. "We dragons were among the first creatures who woke when this world was created."

"And have never stopped bragging about it," Monkey observed.

Mr. Hu stepped between them before they continued the quarrel. "Let's save our anger for the thieves, shall we?"

"I will," Mistral said through gritted teeth, "but if we survive, that monkey is going to be so sorry."

Mr. Hu turned to Monkey. "And don't play the fool. Dragons have long memories. They're famous for carrying on feuds for millennia."

Monkey scratched his curly sideburns sheepishly. "I know, but I can't help it. She fumes so nicely." But the ape was noticeably silent as they waited at the bus stop.

The 30 Stockton was crowded as usual, but through magic or persistence, they forced their way between the humans packed like sardines in the electric trolley. The 38 Geary was only slightly better. As they passed through the Inner Richmond, Tom looked in the direction of his grandmother's house. It was just as well, he decided, that it wasn't near the bus route. He couldn't bear to see the blackened hole that was all that remained.

By that time the bus had begun to empty out and they were able to find seats, Tom with Mr. Hu. "Is Mistral always so touchy?"

"Dragons are naturally proud, and she has more reason than most to guard her honor," Mr. Hu said, "for that's about all that she has since she was exiled from the dragon kingdom. Some of the scars on her body are not from battles but from the time when her marks of rank and honors were scraped off."

Tom remembered the Guardian's conversation with his

friend at Goblin Square. "Because she insulted the king of all the dragons?" When the disguised tiger nodded, he asked curiously, "Why did she?"

Mr. Hu glanced at his friend and then said in a low voice, "Even the Dragon King can never be sure of his throne. He had a general who was very successful against their enemies."

"Vatten's followers?" Tom asked.

"Perhaps, but there are also others who would challenge the dragons for control of the seas. They raid the borders and towns. But this general was the shield against them all." Mr. Hu settled back in the seat. "However, there were dragons at court who were jealous of his honors and told the Dragon King that the general was *too* successful and *too* ambitious, and that one day he would take the throne from the Dragon King. The Dragon King was ever mindful of rebels, and so he had the general executed."

"But that's crazy," Tom said.

Mr. Hu shrugged. "You can look to your own history. There was General Belisarius, who served the Byzantine emperor Justinian. And there was General Pan Ch'ao, who served the Han emperor. Though they were as loyal as they were successful, their rulers turned on them. Dragon rulers are just as insecure over their thrones. It was very unwise of Mistral to tell the high king he was a lazy clown for what he did."

"I would have called that king worse things," Tom said, glancing at the dragon, who sat at the back of the bus.

"And you would have been executed instead of exiled." Mr. Hu began to comb his goatee. The dandyish tiger could never resist grooming himself for very long.

"Why wasn't she?" Tom asked.

"She'd been of service to the dragon kingdom herself," Mr. Hu explained. "It might have been kinder to have killed her instead of banishing her from the sea. She has led a difficult life, so she doesn't trust many. You should take it as a great compliment that she thinks well of you."

They got off the bus at the end of the line. Here the houses were jammed shoulder to shoulder right up to the sidewalk so that the street seemed to be lined with stucco walls. On several homes Tom saw a strange graffiti. It looked like a big number nine but with a curly snake's tail.

"Do you see that?" Mistral muttered to them.

Mr. Hu let out a growl as he stared at the design. "Things are far worse than I thought."

"What's wrong?" Tom asked nervously.

Alert and tense again, Mr. Hu turned his head from left to right as he checked the street. "Vatten's first form was a nine-headed serpent, and that mark became the symbol of his rebellion. His followers still use it. That's why they call themselves the Clan of the Nine."

"But never openly," Monkey said, looking solemn.

Mr. Hu warned, "We have to be extremely careful."

They followed the street until it ended abruptly at a small park on a hilltop overlooking the ocean. A mansion sat in the middle. Tall eucalyptus trees grew around the park's edge, littering the ground with long, pink, fingerlike leaves and fragrant nuts. Now that they were out of sight, they paused long enough for Mr. Hu and the others to change into their true shapes.

Mr. Hu snuffled irritably and rubbed his paw over his nose. "Blast. I can't smell a thing with all this menthol from the eucalyptus. It's like having my nose stuck in a bottle of medicine." He looked around and sighed. "And there aren't any seagulls either. That's odd because there are always some scavenging by the sea."

The tiger started forward purposefully, but Mistral stomped a paw down on his tail to stop him. "You're the Guardian now," she scolded in a low voice, "so it's time to start thinking like one. You can't lead the charge anymore."

Mr. Hu yanked his tail free indignantly. "You ought to know me after all these years. I can't just sit in safety while others risk their lives."

Mistral glanced at the mansion and said dryly, "I believe there will be enough danger for everyone before we're done with Vatten."

"Maybe I should go first," Monkey whispered.

Mr. Hu rubbed the back of his neck in frustration and his tail whipped back and forth. It was obvious that he was fighting his own natural instincts. "All right," he growled reluctantly, "but no showing off." As Monkey moved off with a nod, the tiger ordered Tom to follow him.

It was Mistral's turn to object. "Only cowards are placed in the rear."

"You said yourself no place is safe. We have no idea how our enemies are going to strike," the tiger said. "And if I must forget my pride, so must you."

Mistral dipped her head grudgingly, but they could hear her grumbling softly behind them.

Tom did his best to move quietly, but no matter how hard he tried, he kept stepping on the leaves that littered the dirt.

Mr. Hu's tail grew still as he stared ahead. Feeling nervous, Tom slid in closer.

Monkey was crouching, waiting for them at the edge of the trees. There must have been a lawn once, but weeds now grew almost waist high, their tips bending over with dew. Fat bushes rose out of them like silent green explosions. From not very far away, they heard the crash of surf against rocks.

Mistral raised her head eagerly. "I can hear the ocean. It's been a long time since I've been so close to home." She wagged her tail like a dog. Vatten, it seemed, was not the only one who drew energy from the sea.

For once Monkey glanced sympathetically at the dragon. "The Dragon King's punishment was a harsh one."

"If I'd known how hard exile from the kingdom would be, I might have chosen death instead," the dragon grunted.

"Knowing how you hold your honor so dear, you would have done the same," Mr. Hu said.

Mistral sighed. "But the ocean calls me. The beating of the waves is like the beating of my heart. It was a mistake for me to come this near to it again."

Tom put a hand sympathetically on the dragon's side. "It must be hard to be homesick."

"That's such a tame word for what I feel. 'Come to me,' the sea is whispering. It's in my blood. I've avoided the ocean for just this reason."

"I'm sorry that my need has brought you here," Mr. Hu said, and then offered, "I could put a spell on you."

Mistral drew a ragged breath. "No. The sea is in every dragon. I cannot ignore what I am." Her tail lashed nervously. "But it will take much of my strength."

"Then the sooner we leave, the better. I'll scout ahead," Monkey said. He disappeared into the mist after only five yards.

"What's that?" Tom pointed at a nearby bush where parts of a rusty wire frame showed through the branches.

"It's a topiary," Mr. Hu explained. "They grow the bush and trim it so it's like a statue of something. Only it's lost its shape because nobody's tended to it."

Tom squinted. "It used to be a seahorse."

"It looks like no one's been here for years," Mistral said.

"I would have sworn the spy's trail led here." Mr. Hu's whiskers twitched in confusion as Monkey returned.

"The way looks clear at any rate," he said.

"Then let's go," Mr. Hu said, and turned to Mistral. "If

there's trouble, protect Master Thomas."

The dragon compared her claws with the tiger's. "I think it would be better if you did that." She smiled. "This is no time for a tiger's pride."

Mr. Hu wriggled his large black nose as if he did not relish having his own words thrown back at him, but he shrugged. "Oh, very well."

Though the high weeds and grass hid the ground, it felt fairly smooth as it swept up the slope. Tom gave a cry when he suddenly saw a shape.

Mr. Hu crouched while Mistral plunged ahead. A moment later, she padded back. "It's only a statue," she said.

Tom was feeling embarrassed as they passed the statue. It was of a mermaid sitting upon a rock and playing a harp. The weather had streaked the statue with dirt and softened the features of the mermaid's face as if it was a pencil sketch that someone had half erased. Cold, blank eyes watched them as they left her behind.

When they came to a fountain, Tom glanced over the low marble wall to look at the basin, which was choked with leaves and weeds. Rising out of the basin was a statue of a tall, robed man with a trident, riding upon a shell like a chariot and pulled by dolphins.

They passed several more statues of sea creatures until they came to the mansion itself. Monkey was squatting, almost hidden by the weeds.

The large, two-storied building loomed in front of them.

"This was some place," Tom said.

Patches of green moss covered the stone walls, and the arched windows were covered with boards. The roof itself was slanted sharply, showing gaping holes among the rotting shingles.

Mr. Hu glided silently forward to join Monkey. Lifting his head, he tested the air. "There's something musty," he said finally, "but I can't tell if it's from the ocean or not."

"I don't like it," Mistral said. "I think it could be a trap."

"I'll take a look around first," Monkey said.

As the ape started forward, Mr. Hu grabbed him by the sleeve. "Don't take any chances."

Monkey grinned. "I've never been afraid of a fight."

"And you'll get plenty of that," Mr. Hu promised, "but it won't do any good to have you caught in the thieves' snare. We'd have to go charging in after you."

Monkey squirmed and then shrugged. "I guess it would be better to be careful than to be rescued by a dragon."

"I'd never let you live it down," Mistral swore.

Monkey slipped to the side, circling the mansion. The dragon waited until the ape had gone. "There goes a brave monkey."

"And a wise one, I hope, for a change," Mr. Hu murmured.

Monkey must have circled the mansion because shortly he returned from the opposite side. "I didn't see or hear anything," he said. He rubbed the back of his neck. "But I've just got this feeling."

Mr. Hu tested the air. "This place smells of magic. Strong magic. Something has to be here."

Suddenly they heard a girl cry, "Help me!"

"That sounds like Räv," Tom said, craning his neck as he tried to see. "She's still alive."

He thought of her lying helpless and captive in the claws of the monsters. He couldn't let her die like his grandmother. Before he knew it he was running toward the mansion.

"Come back here," the tiger called after him. "We can't just go rushing in. Didn't I warn you to show some sense about your battles?"

Tom paused long enough to glare at the tiger. "She could be dead by the time we sneak up to the house." He began to move forward again. "If you want to hide like a coward, you can."

"As my apprentice, I command you to return," the tiger said, jabbing a claw at the ground in front of him.

"I'm only a temporary apprentice," Tom snapped as he ran on.

The closer he came to the house, the more details he saw and yet the darker the building seemed. Shadows hung like black banners beneath the gables and arches. Tom wasn't sure what he could do against monsters by himself.

"Help me, someone," Räv moaned.

Though he was more afraid than ever, Tom forced himself up the cracked stone steps. "Räv, where are you?"

"Is that you? I'm inside," she said through the open front door.

Tom stepped onto the porch. "Is there anyone with you?"

"No, I'm by myself," Räv said. "But I'm tied up."

Relieved, Tom started forward, but after a couple of strides, a board creaked under him dangerously, so he stopped. Many of the boards ahead of him looked as if they were rotting away in the salty air. Cautiously he moved over the boards as if he were playing hopscotch.

He saw her sitting on the mosaic floor of the mansion's lobby. Her hands were behind her back, and there was a bandage on one hand.

"Can you stand?" he asked.

Räv struggled to get up and winced in pain. "My ankle hurts too much."

"Okay, I'm coming." He started to cross over the floor. It had a strange design of dogs that were covered with red scales except for their spines and tails, which were covered with coarse blue hair that stuck up like toothbrush bristles.

As he walked over the angry faces, he couldn't shake the feeling they were watching him. Behind him, he heard Mr. Hu and the others crossing the porch. There was a crash of breaking boards.

"Blast. These boards are rotten," he heard Mistral swear.

"Leave it to a dragon to blame everything but her weight," Monkey teased.

Mr. Hu was the first to reach the doorway and he beckoned impatiently. "Master Thomas, come back here at once."

Räv begged, "Don't leave me."

Tom turned, pleading. "We have to get her out of here."

Mr. Hu stayed on the porch. "Have you seen anyone, girl?"

"No," Räv said. "They all left. Oh, they were horrible monsters." She let out another groan. "I need to see a doctor."

"Can't you see she's in pain?" Tom asked angrily.

The tiger twitched his whiskers in annoyance and then nodded to Monkey and Mistral. "Guard us while I tend the child."

Monkey slipped away to the left while the dragon slithered to the right, her claws clicking on the stones.

"I think we'll have to carry her," Tom said.

Mr. Hu sniffed the air. "This place reeks of magic. It's all I can smell now."

"Let's take the girl and go," Monkey said, just as the room was filled with a loud noise like giant stones being struck together.

Suddenly, all around them, they heard cracking sounds. It was like a thousand giant eggshells breaking.

"It's a trap," Monkey yelled. He struggled to leap into the air, but red scaly paws reached from the floor to grip his ankles.

"Get out of here," Mistral said as she also fought to move, but more paws held her legs.

Tom looked down. From out of the floor, he saw a snarling dog rise, its bloodred scales gleaming and the blue bristles along its spine and tail quivering.

CHAPTER EIGHT

The Hsieh look like dogs with scales
and tufts of hair like pig bristles.
—Shan Hai Ching

Tom froze as the dog opened its mouth, revealing its sharp fangs; instead of growling, it let out a wail like an angry baby. The rest of the pack answered in kind so that the room sounded like a nursery full of crying infants.

"Run," Mr. Hu roared as he twisted to strike at the dog that had gripped his hind leg.

"Räv, grab my hand." As Tom started toward her, he felt a paw grab his ankle. Instantly the dog let out another wail and jerked back its paw. Against his chest, Tom felt the charm in the phoenix pouch tingle and grow hot. The dog came no closer. Tom realized the pouch was protecting him, and he tried to head for the girl.

The determined dog rose, shaking the dust from its head and shoulders as it blocked his way.

"Get away!" Tom yelled, kicking at the dog, but it ducked. In the meantime dogs were rising from the floor all around him, forming a wall of crying, furry bodies. Even though they were unable to touch Tom, he still couldn't get around them.

Next to him, Mr. Hu was struggling to break free from the grip of the wailing dogs.

"I can't move," Mistral said, wriggling angrily; all her paws and her tail were being held by the dogs. And more dogs swarmed up from the floor to clutch her neck. The whole pack was rising around them.

"Change," Monkey shouted.

Tom turned to see the ape holding what looked like a metal toothpick in his paw. The next moment it had changed into an iron staff with a gold ring at either end.

He swung it at one of the dogs, but dozens of them seized it in their teeth. "Let go or you'll be sorry," Monkey swore.

With a sudden jerk the dogs pulled Monkey down so that he sprawled on the floor. Instantly more dogs leaped on him to hold him fast.

Räv rose from the floor, her ankle miraculously healed and her hands freed. She had only been pretending to be tied up. "Don't try to fight, Tom, or you'll get hurt," she urged.

He stared at her as she stood in the middle of the floor, untouched by the dogs.

Too late he realized his mistake. "You weren't being chased at all. You're one of Vatten's stooges. And now you were just the bait for the trap."

"And you brought the others in as well," a lazy voice

drawled. "You make a most excellent cheese." Loo rose up beside Räv as if on an elevator. The dogs threw back their heads, but instead of baying in triumph, they made shrill, gurgling noises.

Räv clasped her hands behind her back. "You won't believe me, but I really am sorry, Tom."

"Let the boy go, Loo," Mr. Hu roared anxiously. "Your quarrel is with me."

"It's Mr. Loo to you." He frowned. "My orders were very specific: let none of you interfere with Lord Vatten's plans—which have worked perfectly so far. You let my spy lead you away at first, and now you've followed his trail right here."

"I thought it was Vatten who wanted the phoenix." Mr. Hu's ears flattened against his head as he snarled, "But why did you need your spy to lay a trail if you had Sidney?"

"Why would I hire that detestable little pack rat?" Loo raised a gloved hand and yawned scornfully. "From what I've seen of the new Guardianship, I don't see what Lord Vatten was so worried about."

The tiger lunged so unexpectedly that he broke free of the grip of some of the hounds for a moment. Loo fell backward with a yelp.

Mr. Hu could go no more than a mere yard before the hounds swarmed all over him again. The Guardian heaved and twisted with angry yowls, trying to reach Loo.

"You might have the good grace to accept defeat," Loo said as he stood up and brushed himself off.

"Never," Monkey said.

Loo whirled. "Be quiet, buffoon!" Strolling onto the porch, Loo pivoted gracefully and tapped his umbrella against the boards. Instantly the doorways and windows began to glow with a sickly green light; from above the same light spread over both the ceiling and floor.

The dogs suddenly started to whine in fear. Letting go of their prisoners, they ran toward the doors and windows, but they bounced off as if they had hit an invisible wall. They kept throwing themselves against the openings, trying to break through.

Räv rushed to the doorway and shoved with them. "You can't do this to us, Loo," she called to him.

Loo gave a little apologetic bow. "I'm sorry, my dear. You have no idea how this pains me, but I was told to take no chance of our enemies' escape. The hounds have to remain inside to hold our captives."

"But didn't *I* do everything you asked?" Räv demanded.

Loo jabbed his umbrella toward Tom. "You told me he was dead, but now I find him alive."

Räv hunched her shoulders. "We got what we wanted. I figured we didn't have to kill him."

Loo clicked his tongue. "I'm afraid you have shown too tender a heart, my dear. Be grateful that I'm giving you such a merciful end. Since weakness is a major sin in Lord Vatten's eyes, he would punish you with a death far slower and more gruesome."

"You can't do this to me," Räv said, outraged.

"On the contrary, I can and will; but I'm sure I speak for Lord Vatten when I say your sacrifice is much appreciated. I wish there was time to get a little amber watch fob," he said, grinning wickedly at Mr. Hu.

The tiger bristled and his eyes narrowed dangerously. "Why don't you try?"

"Alas," Loo said, "I must meet my lord." Tipping his hat, he sauntered out.

Räv kept calling and pleading long after he had disappeared from sight. Finally, with one last push at the unseen barrier, she straightened in shock. "How could he?"

"Very easily, child," Mr. Hu said. "Your master cares no more for you than he does for an ant."

Tom stared at Räv angrily, wanting to blame her for this mess, but she already looked so miserable that he couldn't. After all, this was really his fault. He'd been the one to let Vatten's creature steal the rose and now he'd led the others into a trap. "I'm sorry," he said to Mr. Hu. "You tried to warn me. I should have listened to you and not gone inside."

Tom expected the tiger to scold him some more. However, Mr. Hu glanced from Räv back to Tom. "Your grandmother would have been proud of your impulse: to protect the weak. It's not your fault that Vatten's creatures know how to twist that noble instinct to their own purposes."

Mistral was pushing a paw at the invisible barricade, trying to find a weak spot. "You know, Tom, you remind me of a young tiger cub I once met."

"Really?" Tom asked.

"He was just as stubborn," Mistral said, "and just as impetuous, and he hated taking orders from anyone."

"I don't know who you mean," Mr. Hu snapped.

Mistral punched at another spot in the air. "Confess, Hu: If you'd had any other place to sleep and eat, you never would have stayed with Mistress Lee. She tamed you."

Mr. Hu glared. "Have a care, or I'll show you how tame I am."

The dragon seemed amused by the threat. "I don't think quarreling among ourselves is very useful. I was simply trying to remind you that apprentices are made, not born."

Tom hung his head. "But I've let Grandmom down again."

Mr. Hu began to prowl, whipping his tail back and forth furiously. "You're not alone. You heard Loo. This trap was as much my making as it was yours. But I hate being caged." Whirling around in frustration, the tiger slashed at the wall, but his paw bounced backward while the dogs retreated from him.

"Give me room," Mistral ordered. When she thought she had enough space, she lashed her tail hard at the wall. There was a loud thump but that was all. She said in disgust, "Not even a chip. It's dragonproof."

Monkey somersaulted toward the green, glowing ceiling and struck it with his staff, which rebounded back. "This magic is stronger than steel or stone."

Mr. Hu pounced upon the floor, striking with his claws, but the sharp tips didn't even leave a mark. "The floor too."

The dragon had been pounding steadily at the invisible wall. But when she tried the next blow, she splashed water about. "The room's starting to flood."

Tom felt something wet around his feet. When he looked down, he saw a thin sheet of water beginning to seep across the floor.

Frantically the dragon and tiger tried to batter their way out until, as the quickly rising water reached their ankles, they sent up great sheets of spray. With frightened yelps, the dogs retreated into the center of the room, where they huddled, trembling.

Suddenly Monkey gave a cry and stopped pounding overhead. "The ceiling's coming down."

Startled, Tom looked up. The glowing light seemed to be lower on the stones.

"When Lord Vatten wants you dead, there's no escape," Räv said in despair.

The new threat sent the dragon and ape into a frenzy as they tried to smash their way out, but it was nothing compared to Mr. Hu. He had become an angry beast on the roof; but now the tiger was frightened as well. Whether personal or instinctual, the deadly cage was one of his worst fears. Yowling, he clawed at both the floor and the invisible walls until Tom was almost as afraid of the Guardian as he was of the falling ceiling.

Panting, Monkey slumped in midair. "This ceiling's a little tougher than I thought. What about magic?"

Mistral was puffing as well, her sides heaving like a bellows. "We might as well try. Hu, work a spell, will you?"

The tiger was too far gone. Howling both his fury and terror, he clawed at the mansion, and all the others could do was stare. Even the hounds had stopped their frantic pawing to watch Mr. Hu.

"He's reverted to pure animal." Mistral sighed.

"There's no reasoning with him when he's like that," Monkey said, and glanced at the ceiling. "By the time he snaps out of it, it'll be too late."

Tom felt sure that Mr. Hu, who made such a point of being civilized, would not have wanted anyone to see his naked terror. It was yet one more wrong Tom had done to the Guardian, and he felt even more stupid and worthless. Balling his hands into fists, he felt like pounding his own skull. But then he scolded himself. This was no time to feel sorry for himself.

Staring at the frightened, deadly animal that Mr. Hu had become, Tom suddenly remembered his grandmother's last instruction to the tiger: Use your wits, not your claws. Finally he understood what she had meant by that.

Swallowing, Tom reached in to grasp the tiger's leg. "Mr. Hu, Mr. Hu."

The tiger swung his head, flattening his ears, as if he were about to tear the boy apart; but then he saw it was Tom. He swayed for a moment as he fought his own instincts to attack him. He stilled, but even then, he could not speak but made growling noises.

"Mr. Hu," Tom said. "Think of Mistress Lee. Remember her final lesson."

His grandmother's name had its own magical effect upon the tiger. With difficulty the tiger growled, "Yes-s-s." His ears rose. "Yes."

"Thank heaven you brought him back," Mistral said, and then called to Mr. Hu, "We need your magic, not your muscles."

"Yes," the tiger said, rising on his hind legs and glancing about him self-consciously. "Of course, you're right. I'll give it a try."

Tom stepped back, surprised that he had been able to tame the tiger.

Closing his eyes, the Guardian made signs in the air with a paw as he began to chant. They all watched hopefully, but the wall stayed intact.

Mistral shook her head. "Vatten always seems one step ahead of us. He's probably protected these walls with the strongest enchantments."

"We can't give up," Mr. Hu snarled. He started on another spell.

"That's my old tiger," Monkey grunted, and began swinging his staff again.

"Tigers don't have the sense to know when they're done," Mistral said with a grin, and she roused herself once more into trying to smash her way out.

By now the water was up to Tom's waist. Some of the dogs were paddling about, wailing and yelping; but the tiger, the dragon, and the monkey had not stopped trying to break out.

Tom searched the room again. He owed it to them to get them out of this deadly trap. But how? He didn't have Mr. Hu's magic or Mistral's and Monkey's strength, so what could he do?

He'd have to use his brains. While both the dragon and Monkey tried to smash out of the trap, Tom began to study the room for some other way to escape. Then he noticed Mr. Hu leaning forward to sniff the invisible barrier.

Curious, Tom bent over and smelled the water—and noticed the briny odor. Dipping a finger into the water, he tasted it. It was salty, so it must be from the ocean—which would be the handiest source. There had to be a way for it to come in. Like a pipe.

Taking a deep breath, Tom plunged his head under the water, feeling about with his fingers to find the source of the water.

When he rose for air, he found Räv in front of him.

"Why don't you just give up?" the silver-haired girl asked, puzzled.

From the corner of his eye, Tom could see Mr. Hu trying yet another spell. If the tiger wasn't going to give up, neither was he. "I don't care what your master wants; he's not going to kill us!" Tom snapped, and dived again. It was hard searching under the water, which kept rising steadily. The cold sucked the energy right out of his arms and legs.

Tom finally traced the flow to small, finger-sized holes along one wall. They ran its length. He rose in the water, which was now chest high. "I found the way the seawater's getting in," he spluttered. "I was hoping we could block it somehow; but it's coming out of lots of small holes along the wall. There are too many to cover up."

The descending ceiling had already forced Monkey back to the floor, and Mistral was crouching while the tiger tried yet another spell. Mr. Hu stopped and lowered his paws. "What lets something come in must also let something go out." He nodded to Tom. "Well done, Master Thomas. Truly, you're Mistress Lee's grandson. I can shrink us so we can leave through the pipe and cast a spell so we can breathe underwater."

"I'll check out Tom's discovery right away." Monkey grinned. After he had shrunk his staff, he plucked hairs from his tail and blew on them. Throwing them into the air, he shouted, "Change."

The next moment, there were dozens of little monkeys swirling around his head like flies.

"What else can you do?" Tom asked Monkey in amazement.

"Now you've done it," Mistral said, rolling her eyes. "He'll never stop boasting."

"Don't brag yet," Mr. Hu warned Monkey, "you'll use up the oxygen."

Monkey had raised his staff to test the ceiling. "I see that getting wet hasn't helped your disposition any."

"What about us?" Räv demanded, gesturing to the pack of wet, frightened dogs that had clustered around her.

"Indeed," Mr. Hu demanded, "what about you? Should I be any more merciful than your master?"

Räv drew back as if she had been slapped. "You're right," she said bitterly. "Nobody owes anybody anything."

Even though she'd tricked him twice, Tom couldn't help feeling sorry for her. What kind of life had she led as a servant to Vatten? "If you think that, why did you fool Loo at the store and save me?"

Räv pivoted in exasperation to show them her stiff back. "Don't make anything out of it. If it had been a lot of trouble, I wouldn't have bothered. But you were already unconscious. All I had to do was cut my hand on some broken glass and then smear it on you when I pretended to feel for a pulse."

Tom glanced at her bandaged hand. "So that's when you hurt yourself."

She pulled at the bandage irritably. "I'll never do that again."

"Loo was wrong. Mercy is no sin," Mr. Hu said gently.

Annoyed, she wiped at her eyes as if she did not want them to see any tears. "No, he was right. The one time I thought of someone else, I got into trouble. I should have just stepped aside and let this idiot die."

Mr. Hu studied the girl. "No, I don't think you could have. Loo is right in this much: You have too tender a heart to follow Vatten."

"Please, Mr. Hu," Tom said. "I owe her."

"It doesn't matter. Even if we didn't have to repay your favor. We won't abandon even the Clan of the Nine." Mr. Hu's chin sank down on his chest and he closed his eyes. "Now let me concentrate."

Räv kicked one foot back and forth in the water. "Why did you open the door in the first place?" she asked Tom without looking at him.

"Because it's . . ." Tom shrugged. "It's what my grandmom would have done."

"You don't know how lucky you are to have had someone like that." She wrapped her arms around herself.

She looked so forlorn that despite everything Tom began to feel sorry for her all over again. "Don't you have anyone?"

Räv shook her head. "I never knew my parents. I have always been by myself. Anything I've gotten, I've had to take."

Up until then, Tom had always thought he'd had it bad; but at least he'd had his grandmother. "When I opened the store door, you almost looked surprised."

She gave him a funny little half smile. "I was ordered to try to get you to let me in, but I never expected you to do that."

Tom was puzzled. "Why not?"

She stared at him with a distant look as if she were hearing about some bizarre foreign custom. "Because where I come from, everyone is on their own."

"I'm sorry."

"I don't want your pity," she snapped, and turned away from him angrily, refusing to say anything else.

In the meantime, the miniature apes had returned with the news that the openings led into a pipe that went directly to the sea. At the news Monkey began tearing more hairs out of his tail to make tiny versions of himself; but even now, when they were still in danger, he could not resist some mischief. After a whisper from him, the copies flew in a swarm about Mistral's head.

"Ugh, get these blasted things out of my ears!" the dragon said, swiping at them with a wet paw.

"Careful," Monkey said gleefully. "If you hurt them, who's going to guide the children out?"

Mistral dropped her paw with a splash. "I won't forget this."

"Come over here, Master Thomas," Mr. Hu gestured to Tom. The water was now almost up to Tom's chin.

"What about Räv?" he asked.

"Her too." Mr. Hu motioned impatiently.

Tom swam over to the tiger, but as he passed Räv, he noticed she was trying to force her way through the flood.

"It's faster this way," Tom said, treading water for a moment.

"I never learned how to swim, all right?" Räv snapped.

"Vatten's element is water," Tom said.

"But not mine," the girl said sullenly. "Just because you're the tiger's apprentice doesn't mean you have stripes too."

"Can you float on your back?" Tom asked.

"I guess. Why?" she asked uncertainly.

"I'll take you," he said, raising a hand.

She drew her eyebrows together suspiciously. "Why are you helping me?"

"I don't want your death on my conscience," Tom said. "Will you trust me?"

"We are not like your master," Mr. Hu assured her.

Räv hesitated and then turned nervously, facing the ceiling as she lifted her legs from the floor. The motion started to make her sink, but Tom caught her.

She glanced at him, surprised. "The last time I touched you, I got a shock. Why don't I feel it now?"

"He's wearing a magical charm," Mr. Hu explained, "that protects him from evil, but it senses no danger in you now."

"A lot it knows," Räv said.

"Arch your back more," Tom said.

Her hand grabbed his shoulder for support as she obeyed. Slowly her body rose to the surface. Using one hand to stroke the water, Tom towed her with the other over to the wall.

"I don't understand you at all," she said, spitting out a mouthful of water.

"You said it yourself: I'm stupid," Tom said.

"Or very kind," Räv said, digging her fingers into his shoulder in her fear. "Maybe too kind for your own good."

It took Mr. Hu only a moment to draw some more signs in the air and mutter some spells. The next second, the water in the room seemed as big as an ocean as they shrank; and as Tom dived through the surface, the floor seemed a mile away.

Then a paw took his arm. Turning, he saw a miniature version of Monkey holding him. With a wink the little ape began pulling him downward toward the wall.

Tom had been holding his breath all this time, but the distance was now so great that he found himself exhaling. He was relieved to find that the Guardian's magic had worked and he could breathe underwater.

The little monkey pulled him through the opening. They both had to kick to make headway against the powerful current. The swim through the dark pipe seemed to take forever. Then he saw the bright circle of light at one end.

The next moment he was bobbing up through the surf. The cliffs overhead loomed large as mountains and the grains of sand seemed as big as pebbles as the little ape pulled him over to a narrow strip of beach.

A moment later, Räv joined him, gasping on the sand while the little apes returned for the others. "I didn't see any pump to send the water into the mansion," Tom said. "It must be magic."

Then, by the dozens, the dogs' tiny red heads bobbed

up by the pipe intakes. Each had a miniature monkey to help it. The monkeys didn't leave when they had brought the dogs to the beach; they stayed as guards.

Räv crawled over to Tom and just stared at him for a long time before she finally managed to mumble "Thank you."

"Forget it. I would have done it for anyone," Tom said, wiping at the saltwater that stung his eyes.

"Yes," Räv said softly, "I believe you would." She bit her lip for a moment and then added, "Lord Vatten's not going to wait for the phoenix to come out of the egg naturally. He's found a way to force the egg to hatch."

Tom stared at her uncertainly. "Why would I believe anything you say?"

Räv drew back her head. "You can trust me or not. I don't care. But I don't like owing debts."

"If you really want to pay me back," Tom urged, "tell us where your master has the egg."

Räv hunched her shoulders. "He's my master no longer. And as for its location, that secret's worth my freedom."

Tom still didn't know whether she was lying or not. "I'll see what I can do."

Just then, more of the dogs appeared, along with Monkey himself and a miniature Mistral. "Where's Mr. Hu?" Tom asked them.

"He'll be last," Mistral said with an admiring nod.

"There isn't much time left before the ceiling will come down against the floor," Monkey said. "It took such a long time to cast spells on all these hounds."

At the moment, all the fight was out of their enemies. They sat on their haunches on the beach, panting.

"Change," Monkey said, and he suddenly grew as large as a giant.

Tom had an anxious moment before he finally saw the tiger's head break the surface. Somehow the determined tiger had kept hold of his hat as well. "You made it," the boy said, greeting the Guardian at the surf.

He was so glad that he almost hugged the tiger, but Mr. Hu started to shake himself dry. Though his suit had stayed dry because of the special wool, his fur had not and he sprayed water all over.

"Of course I did," Mr. Hu said, as if he did this every day.

When the tiger had changed himself back to full size, the dragon began to hop up and down on the beach. "Change me next before that ape steps on me."

Monkey slapped a paw to his forehead. "I was so busy worrying about the tiger that I forgot. A lizard like you would make a nice pet."

He was just starting to reach for Mistral when the dragon suddenly swelled up to her normal size. "You were saying?" she asked with a smile that showed an alarming number of teeth.

Monkey backed off. "But you make an even better friend."

"I am not now nor ever will be the friend of a furball like you," Mistral said.

Mr. Hu, in the meantime, was busy restoring Tom to his regular size.

"What about Räv?" Tom asked.

"Unfortunately, she will have to remain a prisoner with the hounds," the tiger said, fishing out what looked like a green lump of gum from his pocket.

"But she told me what Vatten's planning," Tom said. "He's going to force the egg to hatch early. And she'll tell you where if you let her go."

Mr. Hu kneaded the gum between his claws as he considered the offer, but finally he shook his head. "She's lied to you twice. Why should we trust her a third time?"

"I have no reason to love Vatten now and neither do the hounds," Räv's voice came up to them, thin and shrill. "He abandoned us to die."

"I promise you that you will feel no pain, only sleep and dreams of pleasant things," Mr. Hu said.

Tom wanted to believe she could change. "Please don't do this to her."

"A Guardian must sometimes make difficult decisions," Mr. Hu said, breathing on the lump.

Tom planted a fist on his hip. "Is that another one of your rules?"

"Not mine, but your grandmother's. Why do you think she stayed behind?" Mr. Hu asked, and strode over to the dogs, who were swirling about anxiously in a restless, red pool, pressing against the wall of tiny monkeys that now trapped them.

Muttering a spell and making signs with his free paw, Mr. Hu held the green lump over them. The red dots rose into the air, yelping and wailing, and were drawn into the lump.

Tom squinted, trying to see Räv, but there were too many of the dogs and then all that was left of them was the lump, hardened into a green rock, which Mr. Hu now dropped into a coat pocket.

CHAPTER NINE

The dragon seemed to have gathered new energy after being in the ocean. She was as frisky as a giant kitten. "Careful," Monkey said, holding up a paw before his eyes. "You're getting sand over everyone."

"I can't help it," Mistral cried excitedly. "The swim has renewed me." She gazed toward the horizon. "I wish I could see the coral palaces of the Underwater Kingdom again. And the Fire Gardens at sunset." Her eyes narrowed as if she were trying hard to glimpse them. "The water overhead turns to red, and the garden itself glows like living flames that dance to the singing of the pipefish. And the pipefish rise in schools that glitter like rainbow clouds."

"You miss the ocean that much?" Tom asked sympathetically.

"The ache grows with each year," Mistral said, gazing longingly at the sea.

In contrast Mr. Hu was feeling the effects of working so

many spells. The elderly tiger sat slumped, with barely enough energy to raise a paw. "Well, not all of us are waterproof. Use some of that vigor to help us get a fire going."

Mistral glanced at the shivering boy. "Yes, of course." She swept the driftwood on the beach into a big pile with her tail and her paws.

"I'll go try to find some trace of Loo," Monkey volunteered.

"You don't want to go out looking like that," Mistral said. "Your tail looks like a rat's."

"Better than having one that looks like a snake," Monkey said, waving the bald, pink tip of his tail at the dragon. "And I was going to go out in disguise anyway."

Once he had restored the hairs to his tail, he transformed himself, hiked up the path that zigzagged up the cliff face, and disappeared from sight.

When Mistral had piled enough wood together, the tiger knelt and, with a muttered spell, soon had a bonfire going. The dragon, feeling in an obliging mood for once, stretched out her body and lay down so that her long body acted as a windbreak for the others.

Tom could see how scarred and dented her scales were. "You've led a hard life, haven't you?" he asked.

"No more than Hu," Mistral said.

"And Monkey," Mr. Hu reminded the dragon gently. "He's been as much of an outlaw as you. That ought to give you something in common."

Mistral narrowed her eyes. "Insult me that way one more

time and I'll leave you, Hu."

"What did Monkey do to become an outlaw?" Tom asked.

"That ape's pride would dwarf the sun," Mistral said. "He actually challenged Heaven."

"And was punished for it," Mr. Hu said. Taking off his coat, he began to roll up his sleeves as he explained. "He was buried alive under an entire mountain."

"Which crushed neither his pride nor him," Mistral complained.

"His pride was all he had while he was imprisoned," Mr. Hu argued. Taking a small jar from his coat pocket, he unscrewed the lid and began to rub an ugly brown ointment on his elbows and wrists.

"Let me do that," Tom said, going over to him.

As Tom rubbed the tiger's fur, he said, "I used to do the same for Grandmom." Pleased, the tiger lay down on all fours while the boy probed and rubbed. The Guardian's muscles were different from a human's, so Tom could not be sure he was doing a good job until he heard Mr. Hu begin to purr, rumbling like a truck.

When Tom was finished, the Guardian stretched out on the sand to rest and regain his strength, telling his temporary apprentice how Monkey had led the other apes in a rebellion against Heaven itself. At first Heaven had tried to buy his loyalty by offering him a minor post. However, Monkey stole some peaches that granted immortality and then wrecked a banquet to which he had not been invited.

Of course, a heavenly host flew down to punish him, but Monkey held his own until the Flower Lord, a strange, terrible wizard, had captured him.

"So he's immortal?" Tom asked.

During the recital of Monkey's adventures, Mistral had closed her eyes and pretended extreme indifference, but she grumbled now, "He may be immortal. Even so, I swear he's lost a step or two."

The tiger had taken the ointment back from Tom, and now he rolled up his pants legs and began applying it to his knees. "Hush, here he comes," Mr. Hu said as Monkey returned.

When Monkey slogged back across the sand toward them, he wrinkled his nose. "Phew, is that stink you, Hu?"

"My joints get a little stiff," Mr. Hu huffed, screwing the lid back on the jar. "And it's good for that."

"Only old grandfathers use that dreadful stuff," Mistral teased, but she sobered up quick enough when Monkey told them that he had lost Loo's trail once he had reached the street.

"What do we do?" Mistral wondered. "Where does Vatten plan to force the phoenix to hatch?"

Monkey settled down beside them. "I think that girl must have been lying. We have plenty of time to find the egg."

"But if she wasn't," Mistral said grimly, "Vatten will wreak havoc even sooner than we thought."

"I think we have to assume the worst," Mr. Hu said,

"which means we have to get the egg back before Vatten can carry out his plans."

"Maybe you should bring the girl out again and accept her bargain," Monkey suggested.

"I don't trust her," Mr. Hu said with a firm shake of his head.

Mistral was alternately scooping sand into the shape of Loo and pounding it flat. "Wherever Vatten is, he must be near water. But we not only have the ocean on this side of San Francisco, we also have the bay on the other. That is a wide area to search if you include the coastline."

Suddenly they heard a faint humming noise from overhead.

"Well, now, Mr. H," Sidney called from above. "Just look at the kind of trouble you get into when your partner's not around."

The tiger glared up at the round rat as he slowly descended from the sky. "You! How did you escape? I tied you up myself."

Sidney chuckled. "I guess you didn't know rats can squeeze their bones close together. That's how we can get through cracks and holes. And as for the vault, well, that kind is designed to keep people out, not in." He patted part of his fur and Tom heard a distinct clink. "And when you've got the tools and the know-how, it's no problem. But I can fix that vault so no one can get out. I'll give you a break on the price too."

Mr. Hu swatted at the rat with his hat. "So you've come to gloat?"

Sidney easily evaded the tiger and settled on the beach. "No, to help. You're my partner, Mr. H. I knew you were just pretending to be mean. You were worried about me so you used that as your excuse to leave me behind. But I figured I'd better keep an eye on you, so I've been flying along up above you all this time."

Mr. Hu jumped erect on his hind paws. "You knew we were in trouble and didn't help us?"

"Between the ape and the dragon and you, I knew you'd get out," Sidney said as he deflated his fur.

Monkey nodded to the boy. "Actually, it was Tom who got us out."

"Do tell," Sidney said, eyeing him. "And he looks so harmless. Well, I followed the guy with the umbrella."

Mr. Hu demanded impatiently, "Where did Loo go?"

Sidney flicked a paw toward the east. "Do you know the big freshwater lake in the park?"

"Stow Lake, sure," Tom said.

"There's a hill in the middle of the lake. He went inside there," Sidney said.

Mistral rose in a cascade of sand. "Then that has to be where Vatten is as well. Clever. He's surrounded by water. I would have wasted my time searching along the saltwater rather than thinking of looking for a body of freshwater in the city."

"And that's where we're going next." Sidney sidled up to the tiger and nudged him with an elbow. "Right, partner?"

Poor Mr. Hu struggled with himself before he said through gritted teeth, "Yes."

Mistral twisted her long neck to stare at the ocean one last time and sighed. "It's hard to leave the sea after having had just a taste of it."

"Can't you come back when this is over?" Tom asked.

The dragon twisted up one corner of her mouth. "I think this may be my last battle. But even if I survive, I couldn't return here. I could not resist the temptation to return to the kingdom if I came to this beach again. And that would lead to my death more surely than even entering Vatten's lair will. It would cost my life to set paw in the dragon kingdom. Even swimming out of the mansion was a risk."

"Oh, now, don't start composing your funeral chant or you'll be here for days. There's nothing like a dragon when it comes to dying." Monkey shrank his staff to the size of a toothpick. "And in the meantime Vatten will be doing whatever he wants to the phoenix."

Mistral still seemed convinced that this would be her final fight. She cleared her throat. "Perhaps the boy shouldn't go with us this time."

After tangling with the Clan of the Nine at the mansion, Tom was not sure he wanted to meet their master himself. "But you're going to go? Aren't you scared?" he asked the dragon and the others.

"Of course," Mr. Hu grunted. "Only a fool would pretend

not to be, and I'm no fool."

"And yet," Monkey chuckled as he tucked his staff behind his ear, "only fools would challenge Vatten and his forces."

Mistral took one last, long look at her ocean home. "Some would even call it suicide—which is why the boy shouldn't accompany us."

"Yes," Mr. Hu said thoughtfully, "perhaps he shouldn't."

Tom scratched his forehead. "Back at Grandmom's, you warned me not to take on a fight when the odds are against me. So why are *you* going after Vatten? You admit he's probably stronger than you."

Mr. Hu stroked the fur along his jowls. "You have a very inconvenient memory and an annoying habit of tossing someone's words back at him." The tiger smiled gently. "I guess it's because there's no one else to save the phoenix."

Tom stared at the elderly tiger. "But you're stiff all the time and you hurt your back when you exert yourself. You're too old to fight." He glanced at the ape and then the scarred dragon. "All of you are."

"Well, now—" Monkey began to protest.

"Be honest for once in your life," Mistral said. "We're all getting on in years."

"Speak for yourself, lizard." Monkey paused and then scratched his cheek. "But," he admitted, "after all these years of wandering and fighting, I thought I'd have more to show for them."

"So you're tired as well," Mistral grunted.

Dragon, tiger, and ape stared at the fire as if they were seeing their own lives in the flames—all the endless battles and travels.

Tom felt as if he had said the wrong thing as usual. Even if it was true, it had been mean to remind them. "I'm sorry. I should have kept my mouth shut."

Finally Mr. Hu made one last adjustment to his tie. "Well," he said with a dignified nod, "if this is to be my last lesson to you, Master Thomas, let it be this: True courage is doing what you know must be done."

Monkey could see how bad the boy felt and reached over to pat his knee. "Don't have such a long face, Tom. This is all that rascals like us deserve."

Mistral suddenly lifted her long neck and laughed sardonically. "Hatchling, learn from us. Don't spend your lives seeking trouble, for you surely will find it."

Mr. Hu grinned crookedly. "I'm afraid it's too late for us to mend our ways, but a cub like you still can."

Tom stared at the tiger, whose quiet courage reminded him of his grandmother as she had stood in the parlor, preparing to make her last stand. The ape and dragon, too, had the same determined air. He felt his heart bursting with pride for the three old warriors. He couldn't hide while they went on into danger.

His Adam's apple felt as big as a melon when he swallowed and said, "I don't know how much help I'll be, but I'm going too." Tom touched the pouch hanging inside his shirt. By now the gesture felt natural. "This charm kept the hounds away from me."

"They were only minor threats. It will not protect you against Loo or any of the greater beasts that are likely to be guarding the egg," Mr. Hu said.

Tom never thought he would have to justify risking his life. "But I found the escape route, didn't I? I can help a little."

"It's still foolhardy to let him come with us," Monkey said to the others with a shake of his head.

"I know the way to Stow Lake," Tom insisted. "I'll get there on my own."

Mr. Hu folded his forelegs. "Your mind is set?"

"You can't keep me away," Tom said defiantly.

"You have your grandmother's stubbornness, I see, if not her good sense." Mr. Hu regarded him almost affectionately. "Well, though I would wish otherwise, I think your destiny still lies with ours." The tiger turned to the rat. "But I don't know about yours, Sidney. You should feel free to leave us."

The rat had hunched down, looking miserable. "But you're my partner, Mr. H. I can't leave you in the lurch."

The tiger gently patted the rat on the back. "You've done enough. Now go."

The rat hesitated, as if he were tempted, and then shrugged glumly. "No, I'll stick by you to the end."

"So, it's one phoenix rescue, coming up," Monkey said cheerfully.

"Or one large funeral," Sidney grunted.

CHAPTER TEN

Stow Lake lay in the middle of Golden Gate Park on top of a hill. With Monkey, Mr. Hu, and Mistral disguised as humans, they made their way carefully along a path through the trees until they came to the road that encircled the broad lake. There were bushes and small strips of lawn by the water's edge. Ducks and mud hens floated on the surface, making a meal from the small fish that lived in the lake. This late in the day, there were no rental boats out and no pedestrians.

From the lake rose an island with a waterfall that ran down its hilly slope, passing an ornate pavilion before it emptied into the surrounding water.

Zigzagging carefully through the trees, Sidney found them there. When he had dropped down beside them, he pointed toward a tall column of spray that fell down the hillside.

"I saw someone go behind there so that must be an

entrance," he said in a low voice. "And there's a sentry on top of the hill."

"Did they see you?" Mr. Hu asked.

Sidney chuckled. "They saw me sell a half-dozen golf balls to the last of the tourists."

"If someone could distract the sentry, I could sneak up on him," Monkey suggested.

"Sidney and I can do that," Tom offered.

The tiger fretted for a moment but gave in. "All right, but be careful. We're close to Vatten's lair. I can feel it."

Tom crossed the street, following the pedestrian path around to the stone bridge that spanned the lake to the island. He loitered, pretending to watch a swan swim by.

As they had arranged, Sidney followed him. "Hey, kid, want some oven mittens for your mom?" He had actually produced a pink pair from somewhere inside his fur and was waving them about.

"No, go away," Tom said.

The more the rat persisted, the angrier Tom pretended to become until Sidney muttered, "Sorry, kid, but we got to make this look good." And the rat deftly kicked him in the shin.

"Have it your way," Tom said, irritated for real now as he dived on the rat. Though the boy was larger, the rat was more agile—and more experienced from dodging so many irate customers.

Tom had just eaten a mouthful of soil when Monkey

strolled down to them, looking very satisfied with himself. "Well done," he said. The sentry was gone.

"Thank you," Tom said, spitting out some grass.

While Tom and Sidney dusted themselves off, Mr. Hu and Mistral crossed to them. "You're going to need a thorough cleanup when we get home," Mr. Hu said as Tom wiped the dirt from his eyes.

Sidney began to search through his fur. "Now I've got some soap that's guaranteed to—" He stopped when he saw Mr. Hu's expression. "But maybe later."

They climbed the crumbly earth of the slope and then moved along the hillside. Monkey and Mr. Hu had no trouble, but Tom and the heavier dragon slipped and slid.

"The point is to surprise them," the exasperated tiger whispered to them.

They managed to make the waterfall without incident. Tom could see where the stream splashed on the blocks below, sending up spray like rain. The water looked like a foamy white curtain.

Mr. Hu crouched, placing a hand on the ground. "This is a place of power. I can feel a channel of energy flowing under here."

"But my grandmom said this place was built in the thirties. It was part of a public works project," Tom said.

The Guardian seemed amused. "That's what's on the surface, but what is beneath here? You humans may have built your toy above the *ch'i* line, but it still flows, strong and powerful, whatever you may do." The tiger took in a deep breath of the damp air. "And this place stinks of Vatten's magic too," he growled softly.

"We have to get the rose back," Tom said grimly. "Besides, he had my grandmother killed. I want to pay him back."

"We all do," Mistral growled dangerously. Dragon, ape, and tiger changed back into their true forms.

"I'll lead." Monkey grinned as he raised his staff.

"Remember: the egg first, then revenge," Mr. Hu cautioned.

"Of course," Monkey said absently.

Taking a breath, he stepped into the waterfall and disappeared.

"Mistral, try to keep him from doing anything foolish." Mr. Hu nodded to the dragon.

"I'll try, but it's a full-time job." Mistral thrust her head into the water, and Tom watched the dragon's body vanish.

Mr. Hu eyed the waterfall with distaste, muttering, "Water is . . . is so *wet*." But he leaped after the others.

Tom felt that, as Mr. Hu's temporary apprentice, he should go next, so he took a step forward and almost tripped when Sidney grabbed his leg. "Mind if I snag a ride?" Before Tom could object, the rat had climbed up his pants and wrapped around his stomach, using one paw to hold the flaps of Tom's jacket over himself. "After all, no sense two of us getting soggy."

"Get out of there." Tom tried to open his jacket again

and shove Sidney off, but the rat held both flaps firmly shut.

"Don't forget to zipper it," Sidney said.

Deciding that there was no time to rid himself of the rat, Tom pulled up the zipper.

"Ouch," Sidney complained. "Watch the fur, fella."

"Beggars can't be choosers," Tom said, and zipped up the jacket all the way, looking regretfully at the huge bulge beneath his jacket. He had wanted to try to make an entrance as heroic as Monkey's and Mistral's, but it no longer seemed likely.

Holding his breath, he stepped forward. Instantly, the water pounded at him, buckling his knees. Instinctively, he opened his mouth to gasp and took in more water. He entered Vatten's lair coughing and spluttering rather than the brave way he had wanted. And he almost slipped on the slimy stone.

A paw clamped over his mouth. "Quiet," Mr. Hu whispered as he dragged Tom deeper into the tunnel.

It was about ten feet high and wide and rough hewn, and a torch guttered and burned, casting more smoke than light. The air smelled stagnant, and the stone floor was covered with a slippery green algae. Slimy steps led downward into the darkness.

Mistral crouched with one paw firmly on the shoulder of the ape, who seemed eager to be off. A blue lizard with dagger-long claws lay unconscious by his feet.

As Tom bent over, coughing into the Guardian's paw,

Sidney began to squirm. "Hey, let me out."

The boy pulled down the zipper again and the rat dropped to the floor. "Thanks for the ride." He padded over to the lizard and began searching him for loot. "This was the guy asking about you at first, Mr. H."

Tom wiped some of the water from his eyes and stared at the damp, green-covered cave. "This looks older than the thirties," he mumbled.

"This hill was built over something far more ancient," Monkey said, touching a wall, damp from algae and the waterfall's spray.

Mr. Hu took his paw away from Tom's mouth. "Are you all right?" he asked Tom, but Sidney piped up.

"Just fine, partner."

Mr. Hu frowned and touched Tom on the shoulder. "And you?" When Tom nodded, Mr. Hu glanced at the lizard thoughtfully. "There should have been more guards here."

Mistral kept her eyes ahead. "Maybe Vatten sacrificed them at the mansion."

"The only way to find out is to go on," Mr. Hu said, adjusting his tie and giving a quick brush to his fur.

As Monkey sprang forward with his staff ready, the dragon yanked at the rat's tail. "You too, Sidney," she said. "We've come for the egg, nothing else." She slapped the rat's paws, and he dropped what he had taken from the lizard.

"It wasn't very good anyway." Sidney rubbed his paws clean. "Vatten must pay cheap."

They followed Monkey cautiously down the steps, which grew increasingly slippery. Tom had made sure he was next to the elderly tiger so he could help him, but Mr. Hu's hind paws managed the steps better than his own shoed feet.

The deeper they went, the narrower the passage grew. As the stairway bent sharply to the right, Loo sprang into their path.

"The phoenix is only for Lord Vatten. Not for the likes of you!" he shouted.

"I'll show you who's a buffoon," Monkey said, raising his staff. He still rankled from the insult Loo had thrown at him in the mansion.

"You should have been more cooperative and died back at the mansion," Loo said petulantly. "Now I'll have to give you a more painful end." And he began to open the umbrella.

As wisps of green mist began to rise from it, Mr. Hu clapped a paw over Tom's mouth. "Don't breathe in the vapors or you'll get sick."

"Don't worry," Monkey said, and began to twirl his staff faster and faster until it was a blur like a propeller. "Watch this, dragon," he called proudly over his shoulder.

The green cloud blew back around Loo, who began to cough.

"How do you like your own medicine?" Monkey crowed. Still whirling his staff, he charged forward. Choking, Loo tried to back up, but he was too slow and Monkey's staff shattered the umbrella, sending the bamboo sticks and paper flying. Instantly, the green vapor vanished.

With a snarl, Loo wrenched a slim sword from the umbrella shaft. "I see I have to do this the hard way."

Metal rang on metal as Monkey forced Loo back against one wall. "You go on ahead," Monkey said to the others as he watched Loo. "You have to get to the egg before Vatten finishes with it."

Mr. Hu hesitated. "We can't leave you."

"The egg comes before everything else," Monkey said. "I'll take care of this stinkbag."

"I hate to say it, but the ape's right." Mistral slid her body behind Monkey's, leaving a narrow space between her side and the rock wall. "I'll shield the rest of you while you pass."

Loo tried to leap around Mistral to attack the others, but Monkey beat him back. "You'll never leave here alive," Loo said defiantly.

"Bold words when you don't have your pack of hounds with you," Monkey said, and swung his staff up. "How are you in a real fight?"

Tom cringed but kept on moving as Loo's sword clanged against Monkey's staff. For all of his confidence, Monkey seemed to be having a hard time, for Loo was giving as good as he got.

"Will he be okay?" Tom asked Mistral as she joined them.

The dragon shook her head. "I don't know. They're evenly matched." She glanced at the ceiling. "I don't have enough room to spread my wings and help him."

Mr. Hu hesitated and then shook his head. "We don't have the time anyway."

"But—" Tom began to protest.

"It can't be helped," Mr. Hu said grimly. "Monkey understands."

"Don't you die on us," Mistral called to the ape. "Or I'll be really mad at you then."

CHAPTER ELEVEN

The po has the body of a white horse and a black tail. From its forehead springs a horn, from its mouth a tiger's fangs, from its feet a tiger's claws. Its call is like a drum and it feeds upon tigers and leopards, for its hide is proof against even weapons.
—Shan Hai Ching

Mr. Hu went first down the stairway, with Mistral still bringing up the rear. The sounds of Monkey's deadly battle followed them as they continued deeper into Vatten's lair.

In small niches on either side of the passage were statues a foot high; time had worn away their features so that they seemed hardly more than cylinders with odd lumps here and there, covered with patches of algae and moss. Then the steps began to twist and turn. At each bend Mr. Hu first tested the clammy air for scents, but he found no lurkers.

When they finally reached the bottom of the steps, they found themselves facing a wide tunnel. Here the lamps were grotesque heads from which masses of long hair billowed above four faces that stared in different directions; flames flickered from the stretched mouths like tongues.

Forming the walls and ceiling were smooth slabs of stone in which blue streaks rolled like waves over the white surface. Filthy water hid the floor. A few feet away the nine-headed serpent had been carved crudely into the wall in a clumsy attempt to claim the tunnel for Vatten, but it seemed ancient—far older than the passage above.

Mistral craned her neck over their shoulders to stare at one of the lamps. "Do you recognize it?"

The tiger gazed at the lantern. "No, but I have heard once of a family who were almost as powerful as Kung Kung. In the great rebellion, they broke faith with the Empress and did not come to her aid." Tom knew there was only one empress in Mr. Hu's mind: Nü Kua. "But neither did they join Kung Kung. Instead, they tried to claim they were neutral, waiting to see who would be victorious. When the rebellion was crushed, she punished them by joining them into one creature known as the Watcher. They were called that because it was impossible to surprise them. And so they were set to guard the most important treasures."

"Let's hope the creature is dust by now," Mistral said uneasily. "From what I've heard of the Watcher, we would not want to meet it."

Remembering his mistake at the mansion, Tom asked, "What about the floor?"

Mistral lowered her tail into the water to test the depth. "It only seems about a foot deep."

Tom wrinkled his nose. "It smells like sewer water too."

"It will take a month to clean myself," Mr. Hu said as he eyed the scummy surface.

But they already felt as if something was gathering on their bodies. Something did not want them there, and they felt its anger pressing heavily against them from all sides. Yet there was no challenge to be seen.

"It's just too . . . I don't know . . . too easy." Squatting, Tom poked at the first floor slab, but it seemed solid enough.

Mr. Hu looked thoughtful. "Well done, Master Thomas. You're learning to be cautious and I stand corrected. We should make sure that there aren't any trapdoors. We should throw a rock ahead of us."

However, though they were on a staircase of stone there was nothing they could pry loose. The tiger turned to Sidney. "What have you got in your pockets?"

"What do you need, partner?" The rat reached into his fur eagerly. "I'll give you a good discount."

"Anything so long as it's heavy," Mr. Hu said, holding out a paw.

"Oh no. You'll damage the merchandise." Sidney tried to back up a step, but Mistral caught him by the scruff of his neck and lifted him into the air.

Mr. Hu wriggled his claws. "It's either the merchandise or you, Sidney."

Sidney kicked his hind paws back and forth idly. "Well, I've been thinking about holding a fire sale. I guess I could give up some stuff—since it's for you, Mr. H." The rat dug around in his fur. "No, that's already promised to a customer. And that's for my mother's birthday."

"Sidney!" Mr. Hu rumbled dangerously.

"Okay, okay," Sidney said. Using two paws, he hauled out a brass spittoon, adding, "But you're going to have to explain to my mother."

Mr. Hu took it in both paws. "Where do you keep all this?"

Sidney folded his forelegs together. "You got your magic, and I got mine."

"I think you're part pack rat," Mr. Hu said, and dropped the spittoon in front of them.

It splashed, bonging against the floor and then making waves as it slid through the filthy water across the stone floor.

Reassured, they stepped down into the stinking liquid. Mr. Hu shuddered. "There's mud oozing between my hind claws."

Even so, he bravely led the way as far as the spittoon.

"Oh, my poor baby." Sidney started to pick up the spittoon to clean it, but the tiger took it from him.

"We still need it," Mr. Hu said.

Sidney covered his eyes with his paws. "I can't watch all this abuse."

They repeated the process several times. On the fifth throw the spittoon sank without a trace.

"Uh-oh," Sidney said, putting a paw over his mouth. "There's a hole there."

They edged up to the gap in the floor and Mistral tested it with her tail. "It's only a couple of yards across."

"Now for the other side," Mr. Hu said. "What else do you have, Sidney?"

"You want more?" Sidney said. Tom could have sworn that the rat had grown pale beneath his fur.

"We have to make sure the next section is safe," Mr. Hu said firmly.

"If you weren't my partner . . ." Sidney mumbled, but he handed over a can of caviar.

When the other side proved safe, Mr. Hu nodded to Mistral. "We'll need to cross over on you."

"I am not a bridge," Mistral said.

"It's for the good of the cause," Sidney said, poking the dragon in the side.

"Are you going to let Sidney set an example for you?" Mr. Hu asked.

Grumbling, the dragon stretched her body over the gaping hole and they scrambled onto the next slab.

There were two more booby traps before they reached a large, low-ceilinged chamber with stained, bumpy walls. It took a moment for Tom to realize the bumps were skulls so old that they were brown with age. Some of them looked human, but many were of such odd sizes and shapes that they could not have been. Water dripped down them in slow trickles, streaking them green and blue and orange with minerals.

The floor, which was raised above the level of the tunnel, was of some polished silvery metal that reflected the walls and ceiling.

Sidney crouched down and tested the floor. "It's all one piece so you don't need any more merchandise," he said, relieved.

A doorway stood on the opposite side.

Boom. Boom. Boom.

"Is that thunder?" Tom asked.

Through the doorway trotted a creature that looked like a horse, all white except for her black tail. A white horn spiraled from her forehead. With her reflection in the floor, it looked as if there were twins.

"It's a unicorn," Tom said, and started forward excitedly.

Mr. Hu held him back. "No, that's no unicorn. She has paws, not hooves. It's a po."

"And look at the size of those claws," Mistral said warily.

"And I can assure you the po's fangs are as long as mine," Mr. Hu said.

The po's chest expanded, and she let out a boom like a large drum. "What kept you? I've been waiting to dine on tiger. It's been so long since I had one that I'll enjoy it—even if you do look a little tough."

"I'll take care of her," Mistral said. "We've lost enough time."

"Careful," Mr. Hu said. "Her hide's as tough as yours. Swords and arrows would bounce off it."

"Let's see how she handles a dragon's claws," Mistral said, but when she took a step forward, she skidded.

"The floor's slick as oil," Mr. Hu said. "Are you sure you don't need more help?"

"I can manage a dozen of her," Mistral boasted. "Just let me fly." The dragon unfurled her great wings, but as large as the room was, the ceiling was too low to let her rise into the air. "Then it'll have to be on foot," she said with a nervous smile. She gingerly slid over the floor, looking as awkward as someone trying to ice skate for the first time.

The po glided easily in a large circle around the dragon. "This won't save you, tiger," she said. "When I'm done with the dragon, I'll come for you."

Careful at first, the others began to shuffle across the floor. Tom had never been very good at skating so it only took a few steps before he slipped.

"I've got you," Mr. Hu said, hauling up at his collar until Tom could stand.

Boom. Boom. Boom.

The po thundered like a huge war drum as she slid from side to side, trying to attack them; but the dragon kept managing somehow to stumble in front of her.

Boom. Boom. Boom.

When they reached the doorway on the other side, Mr. Hu called back, "We've made it."

Free of having to protect the others, Mistral cried, "Kamsin! Kamsin!" and began her attack.

With the dragon's war cries echoing in their ears, the others made their way down the hallway to a bronze door. When Mr. Hu opened it, Tom saw a smaller chamber with triangular walls that rose upward toward what must be a point—though Tom could not see it in the darkness. A four-faced lantern hung from the ceiling on a chain, but though it burned as brightly as the lamps in the tunnel, it cast only a dim circle of light around a small crystal table. On the table rested the coral rose.

The silvery floor looked as black as the night's sky except for the reflection of the table and rose at its center, waiting for Lord Vatten to fetch it.

They tested the floor with more of the grieving rat's merchandise, but the path to the rose seemed firm. "It's all clear," Tom said.

Still Mr. Hu crouched, widening his nostrils as he tested the air for scents and twitched his ears for sounds. "Something's still not right. Sometimes the nose and ears will tell you what your eyes cannot."

"Where's Vatten?" Tom asked, worried.

The Guardian straightened up. "Who knows what part of the world he's in? But they must have sent a message to him. We've gotten here before he did, and that's a bit of luck at last. You wait here."

Tom was more afraid of the dark room than he had been of anything he'd met so far, but he knew it was crucial that Vatten not get the egg. And what had he really done except let Räv trick him into losing the phoenix? Monkey and Mistral were both risking their lives. He had no powers and no magical devices. Only himself.

He was certainly no hero, not like his grandmother or the others. But he had never backed away from bad odds before this. "Grandmom, this is for you," he murmured. Making his stiff legs move, he passed around the tiger and into the room.

"Where are you going?" Frantically Mr. Hu snatched at him, but Tom managed to duck under his paw.

"If there's a trap, I'll spring it," Tom said, forcing himself forward though his legs now felt like gelatin. "Then you can get the egg."

"Come back here!" Mr. Hu ordered.

"Grandmom said a Guardian can't be selfish." His steps grew steadier. "And neither can his apprentice. You're the important one. I've finally found something I'm good for."

In the darkness he never saw the thin strands of hair that crisscrossed the room until he walked into them, and by then it was too late.

CHAPTER TWELVE

The strands of hair felt cold and thin as wires, and they did not break but clung to his body until after a few more paces he was wrapped in them. Instinctively, he tried to step back and felt the hair lift his feet from the floor. Panicking, he tried to flail and kick free, but his body only became more enmeshed.

"Lie still," the tiger shouted.

But more hair shot from above so that Tom felt as if he were being buried by a black avalanche. The less he was able to move, the more the panicked boy struggled.

"Sidney," Mr. Hu said urgently.

"One flashlight coming up, Mr. H," the rat said. Despite the booming of the po and Mistral's answering war cries, Tom could hear Sidney fumbling behind him and soft zipping sounds that kept ending in a thud.

"I know it's in here somewhere," the rat apologized. "I

just rearranged things and you know how it goes—"

"Confound it, Sidney, we need it now." Mr. Hu crouched on his hind legs, his large eyes widened even more as he sought to pierce the darkness.

"I'm looking, Mr. H," the rat said.

At first Tom thought it was a black cloud rolling down from the ceiling, but as it swept past the lamp, Tom saw that it was a huge mass of hair, writhing like a tangle of snakes.

"For entering my sanctuary, you must pay," voices sobbed from above. "You must pay."

"It can't be," Mr. Hu gasped. "I'm coming, Master Thomas." From the corner of his eye, Tom saw the tiger framed in the doorway and trying to move forward, but more strands of hair, almost invisible in the dimness, had shot downward to block him. As he swung his claws in a great sweep, the hair broke with loud twangs.

Locks of hair, braided together like ropes, encircled Tom until he was in a cocoon, and he felt himself being drawn upward into the darkness above the lamp.

"Found it, Mr. H." Sidney slipped the flashlight from his fur and snapped it on. "Creepers," the horrified rat said as he saw the hair strands crisscrossing the room at all heights and angles.

The cone of light rose from the flashlight, above the lamp, to the source of the hair itself. A massive creature clung to the pinnacle of the room like an anemone on a rock by the beach. The back, front, and sides of its head each had a face that was streaked with tears. It was the same head as on the lamps in the tunnel—the Watcher.

It blinked in the light and the four mouths wailed at the same time, "How dare you gaze upon me. For that sacrilege, you will all die!"

Mr. Hu glared up at the creature. "Monster, you should have died long ago. There's no place in the world for you now."

"But there will be," the Watcher chorused. "Lord Vatten has promised."

Faster and faster, Tom rose upward. The lips pulled back from the mouths, revealing sharp teeth. But then Tom halted abruptly, as if an invisible wall barred the Watcher. For a moment the creature seemed puzzled as it struggled to bring Tom within reach of its mouths.

"What stopped it?" Sidney asked.

"I gave him a charm," Mr. Hu said, "but is it strong enough?"

Straining with all its might, the Watcher fought the magic of the charm and lifted Tom closer and closer. He tried to scream, but his throat was paralyzed. All he could do was close his eyes.

"Leave the boy alone. Take me," the tiger roared desperately. As he tried to reach the Watcher, he broke so many of the strands that it sounded as if he were destroying a giant piano. And yet more hair kept shooting down from the ceiling to block him.

"I must have something that can cut that stuff," Sidney said, desperately searching his fur. He pulled out a letter opener. "I guess this will have to do." And the rat bravely padded after the tiger. In his hurry Mr. Hu had gotten a hind leg caught just as he was almost up to Tom. Still he leaned forward, sweeping his claws like scythes, in an effort to reach the boy.

Flashlight in one paw and letter opener in the other, Sidney hacked at the troublesome strands around the tiger's leg. As soon as his limb was free, the tiger shed his coat and ripped off his shirt so that the huge muscles on his shoulders and chest rippled beneath his fur. Crouching, he roared, "I am the Guardian, and woe to any who harm my apprentice." And the echoes of his anger rolled around the room like the judgment of Heaven.

When he sprang forward, at first the strands broke under his momentum, but as he fell deeper among them, they held so that he suddenly hung suspended in midair. He had plunged just far enough for one foreleg to reach the monster.

Trapped within its hair, Tom could smell the Watcher's fetid breath and then there was a sharp pain around his heart. Suddenly his whole body felt on fire and he cried out, "Grandmom!"

With one last, despairing howl, the tiger wrenched his hind legs free so he could brace them against the floor. Grief and anger let the tiger shed years and become as he was when he was young—a furred lightning bolt, fighting now for his apprentice and for the world.

He sprang high into the air and raked a paw at one of the beast's unprotected faces. Now it was the Watcher's turn to shriek in pain. Down plummeted the cocoon of hair that held the boy.

"Master Thomas," Mr. Hu panted to the boy, who now hung limp and silent among the strands. He began to cut with large sweeps of his claws.

In the meantime Sidney had dropped the letter opener and managed to dig out a small hatchet. Grasping the handle in his free paw, he swung it in huge, hair-breaking arcs. "You take care of that thing, Mr. H. I'll get Tom." When the rat had hacked through the last strands, he caught the boy barely in time, but his legs buckled under the sudden weight as he lowered Tom to the floor.

"I got him," Sidney said.

"Get him back to the doorway," Mr. Hu called urgently.

"Be right back, Mr. H." Taking Tom's arms, the rat dragged him to safety.

Mr. Hu's ears flattened tight against his skull and his eyes blazed like a wildfire sweeping through a forest. "Come, coward. Or do you only attack small boys?"

The Watcher had had its fill of the tiger's claws. Turning, it began to shoot strands to trap the Guardian.

"Come down here," Mr. Hu raged as he batted the strands away with his paws. "Fight me."

"You'll pay," the Watcher wailed. "All of you will pay."

The tiger tried to spring upward again, but there had only been one such giant leap in his elderly legs and he kept falling far short. "I cannot reach him again." As he fought to keep from becoming ensnared, he snarled to himself, "What did Mistress Lee say? Wits, not claws. Wits, wits. Yes." As he went on defending himself, he whispered to Sidney for two things.

"Sure, I got them." Dropping the hatchet, the rat hunted with both paws through his fur. Careful to use his body to screen himself from the monster's sight, the rat pulled out from his fur a lighter and a can of hair spray, which he uncapped. "Here, partner. You hit it and I'll light it. But as soon as I do, drop the can."

Mr. Hu took the can behind his back, but with only one paw to defend himself now, strands found their mark. "Nasty cat," the Watcher jeered. Hair, braided together thick as ropes, began to fall around the tiger as it sought to trap him in a net.

Picking up the hatchet in one paw, Sidney held the lighter in the other. "Ready, Mr. H."

"Now," Mr. Hu said. Only able to move one foreleg, he aimed the can at the spiderlike creature and squeezed as hard as he could. A thin plume of spray shot out; at the same time the rat lit it. The gas changed into a streamer of blue-and-yellow flame arcing toward the Watcher—but falling short.

"Blast, it's up too high."

But, as the fiery jet faltered, it fell across the ropes of hair binding the tiger to the monster. Instantly, lines of flame raced upward to the cloud of hair hanging down from the Watcher's head. Hair fell like burning serpents, writhing and twisting, and the monster shrieked as the fire engulfed its massive head.

At the same time the fire had raced down the strands of hair toward Mr. Hu. Dropping the can of spray, the tiger began slashing desperately with his claws to free himself; but he wouldn't have done it in time without the rat, who leaped upon his back and swung the hatchet, hacking the rest of the hair away.

"The phoenix," Mr. Hu said. As clumps of flaming hair dropped all around him, the Guardian tried to leap toward the table but again fell short. With smaller hops, sometimes stumbling, he went on, though fire singed his fur and his pants. Gathering the precious rose in one paw, he staggered back toward the door where Sidney waited with an unconscious Tom.

In the outer chamber the booming had stopped. Mistral limped toward them with a bad gash on her hind leg. "Did you get it?"

Mr. Hu crouched beside Tom. "Yes, but at great cost." Putting a paw to Tom's throat, he felt for his pulse. "His heart's barely beating." He took his paw away, puzzled. "Master Thomas could not wait to be free of me. And yet in the end he gave his life that I might live. Why?"

"He said you were the important one," Sidney reminded the tiger softly.

"No, he was wrong. He was the vital one—because he was the future. And as precious as the egg." Tenderly, Mr. Hu brushed a bit of the Watcher's hair from the boy's face. "I should never have let him come. But he had his grandmother's heart, so he could not stay from the battle. Mistress Lee would have been proud of him."

"I'm sorry I'm late, but the rudest fellow detained me. Did I miss any of the fun?" Monkey asked as he joined the others. Despite his breezy air, his robe was torn and there was a cut on his cheek.

"We got the phoenix, but . . ." Mistral nodded toward Tom.

"I've gotten him killed." Mr. Hu's whiskers trembled. "Forgive me, Mistress Lee. I broke my word to you and to him, for I promised I would keep him from harm."

Monkey slipped off his cap. "He would have made a good Guardian."

"He was meant for great things," Mr. Hu mourned.

Mistral chipped the wall when she thumped a paw against it in frustration. "Isn't there anything we can do?"

"I've never seen venom work so fast." Mr. Hu sighed. "He's beyond healing spells already." The fur on his face began to dampen with tears.

"Then let's make him comfy." From his fur, Sidney pulled out a tiny pillow, which he slipped under Tom's head.

"What about a human hospital?" Mistral suggested desperately. "I hear they have devices that take out all the bad blood and put in good blood instead."

Mr. Hu's head jerked back up. "Yes, a transfusion."

"He's gone beyond the reach of human medicine," Monkey said, shaking his head sadly.

"But not beyond magic after all," the tiger said, growing excited. "The boy needs more than blood. I could give him some of my soul."

"How do you do that?" Sidney asked, puzzled.

"Matter and spirit are one and the same thing," Mr. Hu explained impatiently. "You can give energy from your soul—part of your life force—as well as blood from the body."

"But you've already gotten on in years," Mistral protested. "How much do you have to give?"

"I would give it all for his sake," Mr. Hu said, and looked down tenderly at the boy. "He is impetuous and infuriating, but then so was I when I was a cub. And beneath the insolence lies a heart as noble as his grandmother's. He has sacrificed everything for me. Can I do any less for him? If an apprentice cannot be selfish, neither can his master."

"I like the boy as much as you do, but you're not planning what I think you are, are you?" Monkey demanded.

"*She* would know how to do that," Mr. Hu said.

"*She* is never to be woken," Monkey insisted.

Sidney stared at the ape in surprise. "I never expected anyone to scare you."

"*She* is one of the few who can," Monkey said, wrapping his arms around himself.

"Well, who is *she* anyway?" Sidney demanded.

"The Empress Nü Kua," Mr. Hu said in a low voice.

Monkey shook his head. "Not *her*! I hear she gave orders not to be disturbed. You can't be sure what she'll do if you wake her up."

"I will not let his life end here." The tiger's eyes blazed as he gathered the boy into his arms and rose.

Mistral gave a warning shake of her head. "I wouldn't go to her. What *she* thinks of as a good deed might not be your idea of one."

Mr. Hu remained resolved. "Thank you all for what you have done. But now I take a path too perilous for anyone but myself."

Monkey pretended to search for fleas in his fur while he thought, and finally he shrugged. "I like to see things out to the end. Count me in."

Mistral lifted her head. "Never let it be said that an ape has more courage than a dragon."

"Well." Sidney tucked his paws into his fur. "Business has been a little slow lately, so I might as well try a new sales territory."

"You're always the optimist, aren't you?" Mr. Hu asked with a trace of a smile.

Sidney waved a paw. "My mother told me that customers always buy more when it's sunny, so I always look for the bright side of the street."

"If this works, I'll start looking with you, Sidney," Mr. Hu promised.

CHAPTER THIRTEEN

They returned by taxi to Mr. Hu's store as quickly as they could. The Guardian carried Tom himself. They'd had to travel, of course, in human disguise—except for Sidney—but once they were at the tiger's home, they changed back into their true shapes.

Though the elderly tiger was sore from his battle, he began his preparations while the others helped clear the wreckage from the rear apartment into the store so there was an open space.

"This may be the shortest Guardianship on record." Mr. Hu shrugged. He paused long enough to check Tom's pulse. "Good, Master Thomas. Your heart is still fighting."

However, everyone noticed how the tiger hurried as much as his aching body would permit, stopping only to feel Tom's wrist periodically. Every time he did, he looked more and more concerned.

When they had emptied out enough wreckage and Monkey had fashioned a crude stretcher from chair legs and a blanket, the tiger put on a fresh shirt and his coat, which Sidney had brushed and cleaned as best he could with a washcloth. "One can't call upon an empress in rags, so you'd all better tidy up while I finish this."

While Sidney fluffed up his fur and Mistral buffed her armored hide with a towel, Monkey groomed his fur with a borrowed comb. With a sigh, he fingered one of the many tears in his robe. "I can't do much about my clothes, so maybe I'll just stand behind you, Mistral."

"It might be best if you left all the talking to Hu anyway," Mistral said with a meaningful glance.

Wounded, Monkey placed a paw on his chest. "I've reformed. I'm always on my best behavior now. It's just that people misunderstand."

Mistral poked Sidney, who was munching at a stale bagel that he had taken from his fur. "And don't even think of trying to sell her something, you fool rat. Or you'll wind up as dead as Kung Kung."

Monkey said, polishing his staff, "Anyway, in her time there wasn't any money. People bartered for things."

The horrified rat raised a paw to his mouth. "No money? That poor gal. Somebody ought to educate her."

"For the last time, I'm telling you not to bother her," Mistral warned him.

"She has a quick temper?" Sidney asked.

"She is . . ." Mistral paused while she hunted for the right words.

"She's like a great river," Monkey said, "that spreads across the land in the spring. The silt she brings renews the soil, but at the same time the flood sweeps away houses and drowns people."

For once the dragon agreed with him. "Yes," Mistral said, "she's like Nature. She does certain things because she must and she does not care whether she helps or hurts the rest of us."

"Humans," Monkey added, "like to pretend Nature is like them—sometimes nice and sometimes angry. But Nature is indifferent."

"The kind thing to do would be to help her since she's been out of it for such a long time." Sidney stared at a wall. "Let's see. What would she need?" Even though the rat didn't talk anymore about turning Nü Kua into a customer, he looked alarmingly thoughtful—as if he were trying to figure out how to teach her quickly about currency.

By this time the tiger had drawn a diagram on the floor with red ink. In the center of the complicated design was the image of a creature that was half woman and half snake. He crept around on three paws while he fine-tuned the diagram with his brush.

With Tom on the improvised stretcher, they gathered in a circle about the diagram. "I want you to drum on the floor this way," the tiger said, beating his paws against the floor.

Then, taking his place in the center of the diagram, the

Guardian began to dance on his hind legs to the beat, chanting under his breath as he lurched forward rhythmically in a limping dance.

The tiger's deep growl rose and fell, then shot up again like a rocket and fell like a meteor. As he danced, Mr. Hu began to move his forepaws in patterns that left signs glowing in the air like neon. Whenever his body brushed the lingering symbols, they dissipated in a cloud of sparks. At first the little bits of light darted about like fireflies, but as the dancing went on, they began to settle upon the design so that it burned like molten gold.

Suddenly a warm breeze blew through the room. "That can't be part of the spell," Monkey murmured.

"No, it's something else," Mistral said, glancing up at the circle of pale white light shining on the ceiling.

The circle rippled outward like the surface of a pond into which a rock had been thrown.

Mistral swung her head toward the tiger. "Hurry, the Ghost Cart's coming."

"No one cheats the Ghost Cart," Monkey said.

"I will," Mr. Hu said, and went on with his spell.

They all felt a tingling down their spines as the design shone brighter and brighter, and suddenly the floor disappeared. Blue clouds began to swirl beneath them, and in the mist they could vaguely make out the shapes of towers and armies that whirled away before the details became clear.

Finally there was only the damp, sandy earth that gave off a pleasant smell like a beach after a warm summer rain.

Mr. Hu's legs sagged, and he almost fell but caught himself. "It's done."

"You need to rest a moment," Mistral said, lifting a paw to support the tiger.

Mr. Hu shook her off. "We don't have time," he said, pointing as a pale, ghostly wingtip appeared near the ceiling. His ears flattened against his head and he snarled upward, "Not yet. Master Thomas is mine." Whirling around, the tiger grabbed Tom from the stretcher and sank into the dirt.

"Is that quicksand?" Sidney gasped.

"No, but the earth has changed. Or we've transformed. Hu could tell you, but we don't have time for explanations. Hurry and jump, Sidney," Monkey urged with a glance above him. On one fluttering wing of the Ghost Cart, he could see the outline of a ghostly skull, drifting back and forth in the air.

"Hey, it's like swimming," Sidney said as he floated in the soil.

When Monkey dived in, he lingered near the surface of the hole. "The Ghost Cart's just hovering in the room—like it's searching. Why isn't it following us?"

"The Way to the Empress is no longer properly part of the world," Mr. Hu said. "Sidney, I think we'll need the flashlight again."

"Sure thing, Mr. H," the rat said. Getting it out of his fur, he handed it to the tiger.

Mr. Hu gestured to Tom with it. "I need to lead the way.

Monkey, will you take him?"

"Of course," Monkey said, taking the boy. "How long can you hold the Way open?"

"I'm not sure. We'd best hurry." Mr. Hu turned and shone the flashlight downward. By its beam they saw bricks and stones and part of an old lamppost.

As the dragon began to undulate downward after Monkey and Hu, Sidney made the mistake of holding onto her tail, which whipped him back and forth dangerously.

"Slow down. I'm going to be sick," the rat complained.

"I don't know how long Hu can hold the Way open for us," Mistral snapped. "Do you want to be buried alive?"

"I guess I shouldn't have had that bagel," the rat said, and held on even tighter.

At the higher depths they saw broken plates and old bottles and bits of board as well as brick, but as they went deeper, the garbage began to change. They saw bits of rotting straw baskets and arrowheads and piles of discarded mussel shells and charred wood from fires. Still deeper they went. Sidney gave a yelp when he saw a giant skull glaring at him.

"It's a dinosaur fossil," Mistral said.

"Watch out," Sidney said as he swam into a rib whose point was still sharp. But he was grateful to see that he passed right through it.

And then they were all blinking and ducking instinctively as they went through what once had been the floor of an ancient sea. Here shells had gathered and fossilized by the thousands and it was reflex to try to avoid them, though they could not feel them.

Descending through the sandy soil was easy, but the lower depths were rock, which resisted them. Both the tiger and monkey looked as if they were trying to swim through thick mud and even the dragon began to breathe heavily.

Finally they came to a chamber with walls of some strange smooth stone streaked with blue, red, white, black, and yellow.

Within the swirls of color, they thought they saw faces—some of them human and some so monstrous that even Mr. Hu shuddered. And there were shapes like trees in parks but others that were plants with tentacles.

Sidney was so busy trying to see pictures in the patterns that he stumbled. The floor, like the walls and the ceiling, was not flat but lumpy, and the slick surface made it easy to slip.

Before them was a set of great bronze doors, green with age. The halves formed the split face of a great scowling beast; its eyes, eyebrows, mouth, and cheeks were shaped by other creatures that seemed to wriggle as if alive.

"Beware," the beast from the doors growled in a deep voice. "The Empress sleeps after her great labors for the world. Do not disturb her slumber."

Mr. Hu, however, stood his ground.

"The Guardian of the Phoenix has an urgent request for the Empress," he said with a bow, and then held up the coral rose.

The beast gazed at the rose as if it could see right through the disguise. "Be it on your heads," the beast finally said, and with a loud groan the doors swung open. Instantly flame rose from rhinoceros-shaped lamps on the walls within.

Inside, they felt a presence so strong that it was almost heavy—as if it were a thick fur coat wrapping itself around their minds and bodies. It wasn't hostile like the Watcher, but it wasn't benevolent either. This was . . . almost indifferent—just as Mistral had said.

They entered a chamber that was shaped like a beehive. The walls were of the same colorful stone as the tunnel, but instead of being smooth, the walls were covered with strands of bumps, almost like cords.

To one side sat a chariot gray as a storm but with bright stripes of gold like lightning bolts. In front of the chariot was a team of four dragons. Two with wings lay on the inside while a pair of green, hornless dragons rested on the outside.

"Are they statues?" Sidney asked, reaching out to touch one.

Mistral batted his paw hand away. "No, but in such a deep slumber that it's like death. Sleep on, brothers and sisters, and dream gentle dreams."

The dragons' harness was not of leather but of some kind of yellow vapor. Its outline kept shimmering and shifting as they watched. The bed within the center of the chamber was also of the same mist.

Upon the bed, looking almost as if she were napping

upon a cloud, lay a girl of about sixteen in a gown of iridescent golden scales. Her black hair was coiled, rising like a tangle of snakes above her head.

Setting down the flashlight, Mr. Hu nodded for Monkey to lay Tom down on the floor. Kneeling, the tiger took off his coat and made a pillow of it for the boy's head. Then, holding the rose in a paw, he bowed.

Careful to stay behind Mistral, Monkey was doing the same; Sidney was keeping close to them. For once, all his greedy thoughts were replaced by fear.

With his forehead still against the floor, Mr. Hu said politely, "The Guardian of the Phoenix begs an audience with you."

When the girl remained lying still, Mr. Hu repeated himself again and then a third time.

"Yes, yes, I heard you the first time," Nü Kua grumbled, opening her eyes. Even though she had spoken in a low tone, her words resonated within them, almost as if their bodies were trumpets through which someone was blowing notes. Sitting up, she started to yawn and put a ringed hand to her mouth. "Why are you pestering me? Haven't I done enough for the world?"

"I have need of your great wisdom and guidance," Mr. Hu said.

"Oh, do straighten up," Nü Kua said, yawning again. "We're not in my throne room so we don't have to stand on ceremony. And it's harder to understand you when you talk into the floor like that."

"Thank you," Mr. Hu said, lifting his head.

"That's better," Nü Kua said, swinging her legs from the bed. "Now be quick about it. Has Kung Kung risen from the dead?"

"No, but his followers are still trying to steal the phoenix egg," Mr. Hu said, and told her briefly about the events of the last few days.

Nü Kua kicked her feet back and forth. "I admit it's serious, but there should be plenty of creatures around who can handle those kinds of things. I don't see why you came here to pester me."

"In the fight, my apprentice was mortally wounded." Mr. Hu nodded down to Tom.

When Nü Kua jumped off the bed, she wobbled as if she had not stood up in a long time and had to put out her arms to balance herself. Little bits of the yellow vapor clung to her ankles like misty anklets. With each step, she grew stronger until she was striding to the injured boy and the anklets had become solid gold.

She felt the pulse in his wrist and then, opening his mouth, she sniffed at his breath. "His time is done, Guardian. He's beyond healing."

"But not beyond sharing," Mr. Hu said, dipping his head respectfully.

Nü Kua glanced at him, startled. "You would willingly give some of your life to him?"

"He gave his life for me," Mr. Hu explained affectionately. "I owe him a debt."

A smile teased Nü Kua's lips as if the elderly tiger's words were only an infant's chatter to her. "Such payment should be made out of love, not obligation."

Mr. Hu gave a little shake of his head. "Please don't talk about love. He will leave me as soon as he is well. But I *must* keep my oath to keep him alive."

"If he had not come to feel love for you, he would not have made the sacrifice in the first place," Nü Kua said gently. "And if you did not feel love for him, you would not be here now."

The tiger looked thoughtful, almost as if he wanted to believe her, but then he spread his paws. "All we have in common is a love of his grandmother."

Nü Kua pursed her lips. "But then you came to see a bit of her in each other and perhaps came to care for that. And caring became love—whether you knew it or not."

Mr. Hu pondered the strange empress's words and then looked down tenderly at the boy. "I think this cub may have taught me a greater lesson than anything I have ever taught him."

"Then," Nü Kua pressed, "if you truly love him, do not do this."

Puzzled, Mr. Hu said, "But I must. In the short time I have known him, he has come to be as precious to me as the phoenix." It had been so hard to admit before, so easy now.

Nü Kua's eyes were golden slits and they gazed at him intently. "Precious, indeed. But are you thinking with your head as well as your heart?"

"I'm not afraid of the sacrifice," the tiger insisted proudly.

"I was thinking of the boy." Nü Kua folded her arms patiently. "Have you considered what will happen to him if you bring him back from death this way? You are of a different species, but if I do this, he will combine yours with his."

"And have the virtues of both," Mr. Hu said confidently.

"I have not always slept. Sometimes I have watched the world." The Empress gestured to a large, circular bronze mirror. "I have seen terrible things done for the wrong reasons, but I have seen even worse done for the right ones. I think your apprentice may come to regret your keeping him alive." Though Nü Kua's face was as youthful as ever, her strange eyes held a great wisdom—and a deep sadness because of that wisdom. "One last time, I warn you: Let him go, Guardian."

"I . . . I cannot," Mr. Hu choked.

Nü Kua turned her gaze from the tiger to the wall as if studying the patterns there.

"Very well." She nodded. Resting her arms against her sides, she began to sway slowly back and forth, whispering a sibilant chant until her whole body seemed limbless—as if her arms and legs had fused together. She curled and straightened like a golden flame. Suddenly she began to drift in circles around the Guardian like a serpent sliding across a floor. The hem of her scaled dress hissed on the floor in counterpoint to her chant.

Monkey, Sidney, and even the dragon could feel their bodies swaying in time to the spell as if this magic was so primeval it called deeper than flesh and bone, commanding the very cells of their bodies.

Finally, with one last swirl, Nü Kua stopped and took a jade dagger from her belt. "Give me your wrist."

Mr. Hu crept over respectfully until he was beside her and then, setting down the rose, held out a forepaw. "Thank you."

"But will the boy thank me or curse this day?" Lifting Tom's wrist, she murmured a spell that did not seem to have any words, just sounds, sometimes harsh and guttural, sometimes rising in a lilt like a bird soaring through the air.

Then, with her dagger, she made a quick slit in both the tiger's and boy's wrists and pressed them together. "Say these words: With my blood, I join you."

"With my blood, I join you," the tiger intoned solemnly.

"Now blow into the portal I have opened," she commanded.

Bending over, Mr. Hu breathed upon the bleeding cut.

"With my breath, I bind you," she said.

"With my breath, I bind you," Mr. Hu repeated.

Nü Kua turned and gestured to Mistral. "You, dragon,

grasp his arm like so." She wrapped her fingers higher up on Tom's arm to stop the flow of blood.

Mistral hurriedly obeyed.

Then Nü Kua nodded to Monkey. "And you, ape. Tear up your robe for bandages."

Frightened, Monkey began to rip up his clothes immediately.

With their help Nü Kua bound up the wounds of both the tiger and the boy. Then she swung her strange gaze toward Monkey, Mistral, and Sidney. She stared at them so long that even Mistral began to squirm. "Yes, nice to see you again." She rose then and waved her hand as if she were shooing away pigeons. "Now let me rest until our next meeting."

"You have a foreseeing?" Mr. Hu asked, resting his cut forepaw against his stomach.

She smiled mysteriously. "Call it destiny. My life has been intertwined before with all of yours." She plucked a shining scale from her gown and pressed it against Tom's cheek, where it clung. "Tell the boy that when he has need of me, he must plant this in the earth, slap the ground, and call my name. I will come." Then, returning to her bed, she lay down, clasping her hands over her stomach. "So farewell until the next time."

And closing her eyes, she fell into a deep slumber again.

CHAPTER FOURTEEN

"What did she mean?" Sidney whispered, glancing nervously at the resting empress. "I've never met her before."

"Me neither." Monkey shivered as he spoke in a hushed tone. "I'd have remembered someone like her."

Mistral touched the glittering scale on Tom's cheek. "I, for one, don't want to see her again."

"You would have to be as desperate as I was, and yet I would never have expected such a privilege. Somehow Master Thomas was important to her in another life," Mr. Hu said, and then staggered as he tried to rise. "I'm afraid this whole affair has left me a little dizzy."

The dragon caught him with her paw. "Who wouldn't be after giving up some of their soul?"

"Mistral, the egg." Mr. Hu waved feebly.

"We'll take care of everything," she promised as she

passed Mr. Hu over to Monkey to lead into the tunnel.

While Mistral got Mr. Hu's coat and tucked the phoenix's egg into a pocket, Sidney snatched up the flashlight. "I have to take the boy," Mistral said to the rat. "Don't you dare go through the pockets."

"Steal from a partner? Never," Sidney said indignantly as he took the coat.

Gathering up the sleeping Tom, Mistral brought him from the chamber while Sidney followed. They all looked relieved when they were standing outside Nü Kua's chamber.

The rat had barely snapped on his flashlight before the doors slammed shut behind them with a clang. In the beam of light, he saw the sign hanging against the bronze. He wrinkled his forehead as he looked at the series of little pictures. "Is it like a comic book?"

"No, it's the ancient script. Every picture is a word," Mistral said, adjusting her grip on Tom.

"What's it say?" Sidney asked.

"A short translation would be: 'Do Not Disturb,'" Mistral said after studying it.

"And the long version?" the rat wondered.

"It's a list of terrible but very inventive punishments if you do," Mistral said.

Sidney gulped as he helped Mr. Hu put on his coat. "But she wouldn't really carry them out, would she? I mean, she sort of knew us."

Monkey nudged the rat. "Let's not find out."

As the rat tried to move to the front with his flashlight, he noticed that his paws stuck to the floor. "Hey, what gives? The stone's gotten soft."

Monkey's foot made a noise when he lifted it. "It's like melted candy."

Mr. Hu sagged against him. "It's hard to hold the Way open."

"We'd better hurry," Mistral said, nodding to the rat to grab hold of her again.

As they fought their way back up to the surface, they found that hurrying was difficult even for the dragon; the stone seemed to have gotten thicker so that it was like trying to swim through glue.

"Hey, it's starting to stick," Sidney said, wiping away stone with the consistency of bread dough.

"Tell me about it," Mistral said. The dragon's scales were half covered in the goo. She was having the most trouble, as the rock solidified around her. Finally she puffed, "Take Tom and save yourselves."

"We wouldn't leave you now any more than we would Tom," Sidney said. If this had been on the land, the rat would never have had a chance of pulling the massive dragon; but the earth was still more liquid than solid. Sidney took one of the dragon's forelegs and began to kick. Somehow the rat managed to help Mistral keep rising up to the layers of sand.

Even here, the going was not as easy as the last time, for the sand was also hardening and with it the fossil shells. The group bruised and scraped themselves as they moved through them. Finally their progress was more like digging than swimming, and it was hard for all of them to breathe. As the ground grew more solid, it became harder to see the others.

"It's just a little more," Monkey called from above. "I've reached the store with Hu."

"Any moths?" Mistral shouted.

"No, but the doorway is shrinking," Monkey said. Even so, the brave ape plunged back to give them a hand with Tom. They emerged from the floor to see Mr. Hu waiting for them.

As Mistral crawled away from the hole, she collapsed. "That was close."

Sidney gave a yelp as the hole shut with a pop on the tip of his tail, which he had carelessly let dangle into it. "It was a lot closer for some of us."

"I'm sorry," Mr. Hu said as he sat down heavily on a chair. "I was so tired that it was hard to focus."

"You need to rest, Mr. H," Sidney said as he helped the tiger off with his coat and hung it on the back of the chair. Snapping off his flashlight and returning it to his fur, he examined his tail for damage.

Mistral lay Tom back down on the stretcher and nodded at Monkey. "In the meantime, this furbag and I will see to things."

Monkey took out his staff but he said, "I don't think

we'll be enough. Now that we have the rose again, Vatten will be coming after us with all his forces. We need a refuge."

"Nonsense. I'll be all right." Mr. Hu struggled to stand up but plopped back down on the seat. "In a little while."

Mistral tried to brush some of the sand from her scales. "Where can we go?"

Monkey rested the staff upon his shoulder. "To the dragon kingdom. The egg will be safe there."

Mistral sank her chin against her chest while she thought about it before she looked back at them. "For once I think the ape is right. The egg should be taken to the dragon kingdom for now. And the sooner the better."

Mr. Hu turned to look at Tom on his stretcher. "Yes, but we'll have to wait until he's stronger. We can't leave him to be taken hostage."

Monkey clapped the dragon's leg affectionately with his paw. "And then you'll get your wish. Our paths are finally going to part."

"You're always trying to tell me what to do, furbag," Mistral snorted. "Maybe that choice should be mine."

"But it would be death for you to go there," Mr. Hu protested.

"I think the phoenix will be my token of safe passage," Mistral said.

"But what if it isn't?" Monkey insisted. Despite all his teasing, he looked worried for Mistral.

The dragon's long neck bent downward. When she

raised her head, it was with a smile. "It's already too late. I've had a taste of the sea again. I am weary of the hardness of the land with its rocks and dust, where the sun sucks the moisture from your scales. I would return again even if this must be the last time. And perhaps before I die I might be able to say enough to gain you the dragons' protection. Though I have been outlawed, there are still many who think well of me."

Mr. Hu shook his head. "This is not the kind of sacrifice a friend can ask of another."

Now that her mind was made up, Mistral seemed almost buoyant. "To quote Tom, 'I know the way.' I'd like to see how either of you can stop me from going." She nudged Monkey with her tail. "But it will be almost as dangerous for this furbag of a thief. Maybe he should stay here."

Monkey looked at the dragon with new respect, but he couldn't resist teasing. "And let you hog all the glory?"

Tom stirred on the stretcher. "Mr. Hu . . ." He propped himself up on an elbow. "The egg!"

Mr. Hu took it from the pocket of his hanging coat and held it up so the light shone off the red petals of its disguise. "We have it."

The boy felt his chest. "The last thing I remember is the Watcher. It was so painful. How did we get here?"

They told him everything that had happened, including the decision to retreat to the dragon kingdom. "You've got a little of the tiger in you now," Monkey finished. "So better be careful when you go past a fish shop."

"You did that for me?" Wondering, Tom turned to Mr. Hu. He had thought only his grandmother would make that kind of sacrifice for him.

Mr. Hu clasped the boy's hand in his paw. "When your grandmother took me as her apprentice, she became like a parent to me. I can do no less for you." Suddenly the tiger looked sad. "Even if you can't wait to escape me."

Tom stared up at the tiger in amazement. "You still want me? But you ought to be glad I want to leave after what I cost you."

"I'll try to be as patient with you as your grandmother was with me," Mr. Hu said hopefully. "And as a Guardian, I will make my share of mistakes, so you must be as patient with me." His head drooped suddenly, but Tom sprang quick as a tiger from the stretcher to catch the Guardian before he fell out of his chair.

"Are you all right?" the boy asked, feeling how much the tiger was leaning on him for support. He now was as energetic as the tiger was exhausted.

"Yes, I just need a little rest," Mr. Hu said, barely able to lift his paw.

"How are you, Tom?" Monkey asked. "You were pretty sick until *she* worked her magic."

Tom touched the scale on his cheek and found it wouldn't come off. From the others' descriptions, he was glad he had slept through his meeting with Nü Kua. "I feel like I could run around the block," he said.

"No wonder," Mistral said, as pleased as any of them to see the boy so lively. "It's all that tiger energy in a small human body."

Sidney, in the meantime, had been making himself at home by rummaging around in the refrigerator. "So what do you say, Tom? My partner and me'll need all the help we can get."

Tom was sure Vatten had even deadlier creatures than the ones they had met, and he had gotten back the egg. So he was free to walk away. But even though he finally had his wish, he could feel how the tiger was leaning on him more and more. He couldn't desert Mr. Hu when he was so weak—not after the tiger had proved how much he cared about Tom.

"I still don't know if I want to do this all my life," Tom said thoughtfully, "but until the phoenix is safe from Vatten, I guess I should go." Once he'd said that, he felt sure it was what his grandmother would have wanted him to do.

"Hear that, Hu," Monkey teased the tiger. "I think you're on probation."

Mr. Hu chuckled. "An imperfect apprentice for an imperfect Guardian. But I suppose it's to the dragon kingdom for all of us."

"But food first," Sidney said, thrusting up a sausage like a sword.

Monkey cleared his throat. "Say, Hu, you wouldn't happen to have any of that ointment?"

As weak as he was, the tiger could not resist teasing. "Even if it stinks?"

Monkey slowly rotated an arm as if trying to work out the kinks. "Unlike that boat the dragon calls a snout, my pert nose is too tired to smell anything."

Mistral gave an embarrassed cough. "Now that the ape brought it up, I could use some of it too."

Mr. Hu savored his revenge. "My, how you've aged. You did say only old people use it."

The dragon coiled up her body so she could rub her spine. "My back's bothering me, and you know what a problem that can be for a dragon."

"You'd need ointment by the gallon," Monkey jeered.

"Fortunately I bought it by the case," Mr. Hu said, and directed them to a closet.

Sidney emptied the contents of the refrigerator and cooked the food quickly. It made Tom feel sad and a little guilty to see how much trouble Mr. Hu had lifting a dumpling to his mouth now. Even so, the tiger refused his help. "I'm not an infant."

Tom hesitated. "Then why have you spilled soy sauce on your vest?"

Mr. Hu looked down, annoyed. "I'll have to soak that immediately or it will be ruined."

"I can do that," Tom said.

Mr. Hu hesitated and then nodded. "Fine. And you'll find my spare vest in the second drawer from the top of the chest."

Tom picked up Mr. Hu's chopsticks. "But first you'll need some lunch."

The fur bristled around the tiger's neck. "I can feed myself."

Mr. Hu didn't scare the boy now. "You've got to keep up your strength," Tom said.

Monkey tossed a shrimp dumpling into his mouth. "Oh, do what he says, you old grump. You're twice as touchy when you're hungry."

"Humph," the tiger huffed, "since when does the Guardian take orders from his apprentice?" But he motioned with a paw. "No, not the pork dumpling. The beef ball."

Tom dropped the rejected item and picked up the desired delicacy with a grin. "Open wide now."

Mr. Hu narrowed his eyes suspiciously. "If I didn't know better, I'd say you were enjoying ordering me around."

"Face it, Hu. You're better at giving commands than taking them." Mistral laughed.

"Well, of course." Mr. Hu's frown turned to a smile. "But I guess I can learn temporarily."

"Teach an old tiger new tricks?" Tom asked with the beef ball poised before the tiger's muzzle.

"Miracles can happen," Mr. Hu said, and stretched his jaws open, exposing sharp fangs.

The sight didn't intimidate Tom because he knew now the tiger would never hurt him. Dumping the food neatly into the Guardian's mouth, he swung his chopsticks back toward the bowl. "So what would you like next?"

"The fish ball, I think." Mr. Hu pointed weakly with a claw. As Tom found the right item, the tiger added in a mumble, "And thank you."

"It's the least an apprentice can do." Tom grinned back.

As Mr. Hu ate, Tom heard the big tiger begin his deep, rumbling purr. Standing next to him, Tom could almost feel the vibrations of the Guardian's contentment.

They were headed for dangerous times ahead, but he'd already gotten Mr. Hu to obey him, and that was a harder challenge than coming back from the dead. Maybe being an apprentice wasn't going to be so bad after all.

AFTERWORD

As a child, I read a good deal of fantasy, but it was Western fantasy, so I was always puzzled by the way dragons were portrayed as evil. In San Francisco's Chinatown I learned that dragons were good creatures that brought the rain. I think that's what first made me aware that I had a dual heritage as a Chinese American, and in time dragons came to symbolize that identity for me.

However, there are other ways in which Chinese mythology differs from Western legends, including those about the phoenix. I was struck by the fact that the Chinese phoenix had the power to change bad creatures. I wondered if the reverse were true: if a phoenix would also have the power to change good creatures. That was the seed from which this book grew, though the Guardians who protect the phoenix are my own invention as are Kung Kung's attempts to use it.

I have also thought it was curious that the first rebel in

the Chinese creation myths was the Minister of Punishment, Kung Kung. I would have expected him to be the opposite: to maintain order and be the one who was most obedient to Heaven's will. However, the myths state Kung Kung was far too strict and rebelled when he was told to be more tolerant.

Many of the fantastical creatures come from legend or that ancient Chinese compendium of wonders, the *Shan Hai Ching* (ca. third century B.C.). Monkey, of course, is drawn from the many tales collected in *The Journey to the West*.